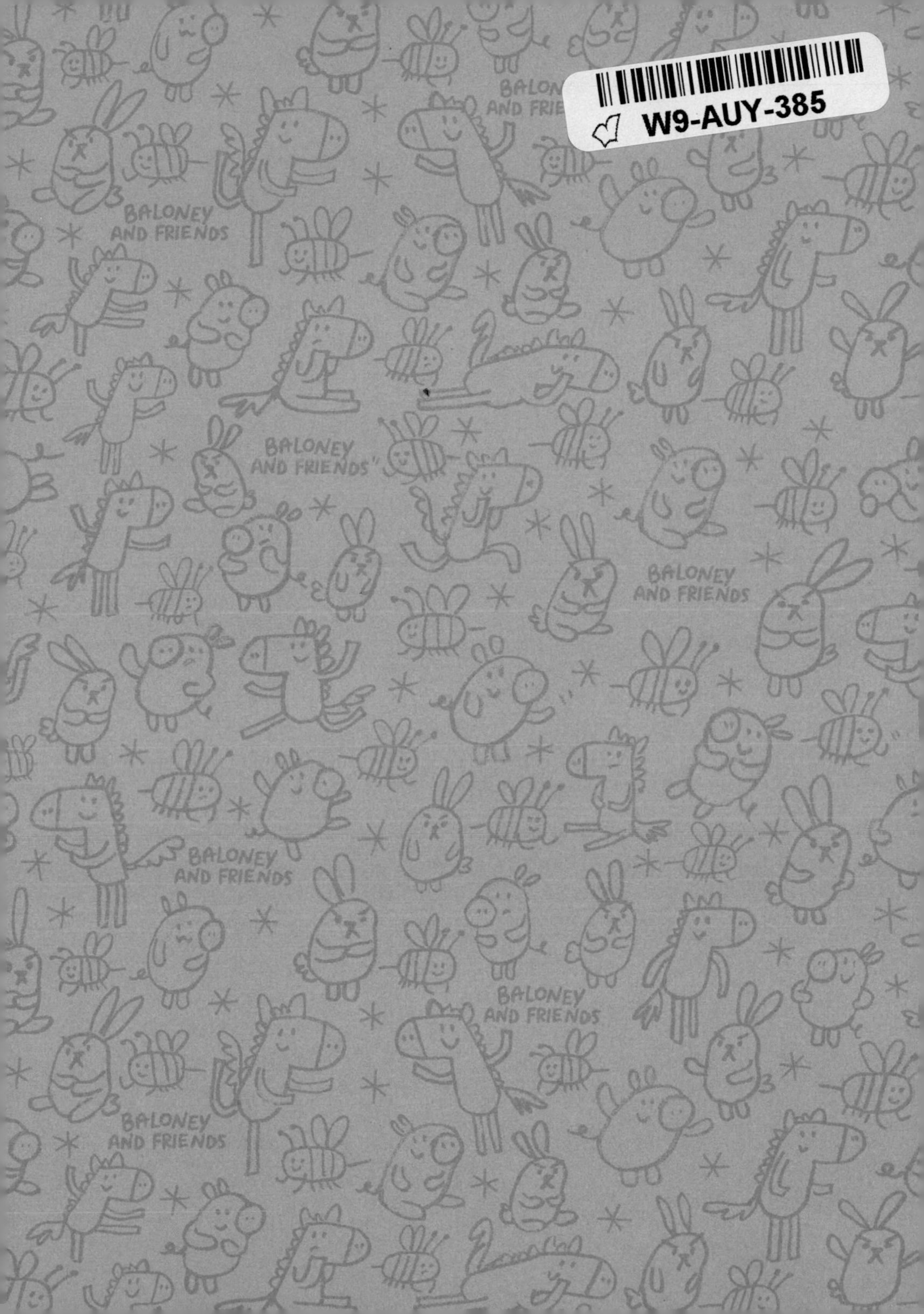
BALONEY
AND FRIENDS

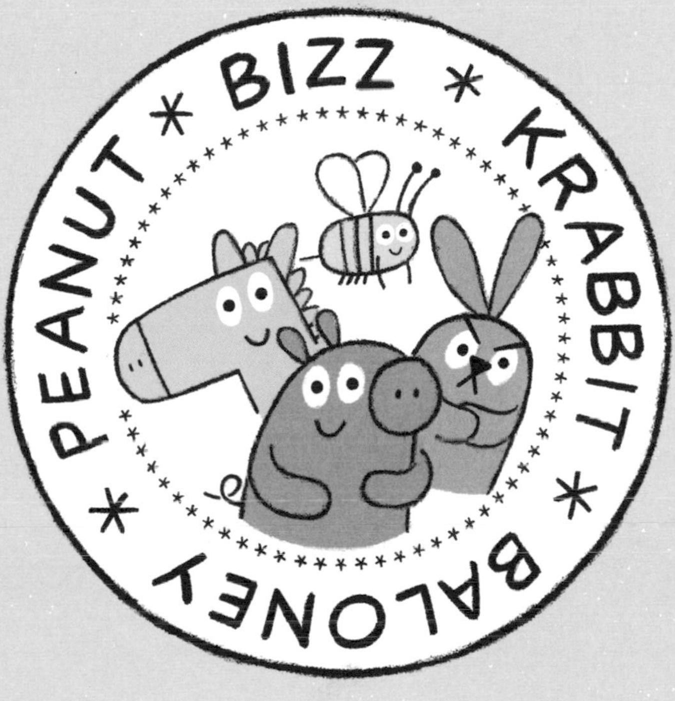
PEANUT * BIZZ * KRABBIT * BALONEY *

FOR ELINE, ANDY, MILO, AND ILYA

Special thanks to my editor, Rotem; to my art director, Joann; to Dina, Heather, Tracey, and all of my friends at Disney • Hyperion; to my wife, Kay, for patiently reading every draft; to Andrea for encouraging me to "just start"; to Steve for telling me to "keep going"; and to Dav, Ryan, and Patrick for their kindness along the way. And extra special thanks go to the Lower School Girls of Springside Chestnut Hill Academy, who saw the book in early sketches and were very helpful.

First Edition, April 2020
10 9 8 7 6 5 4 3 2 1
FAC- 029191-20059
Printed in Malaysia
Hand-lettering by Greg Pizzoli
Library of Congress Control Number: 2019945148

ISBN 978-1-368-05454-6
Reinforced binding
Visit www.DisneyBooks.com

BALONEY
AND FRIENDS

GREG PIZZOLI

DISNEY · HYPERION

LOS ANGELES   NEW YORK

TABLE OF CONTENTS

BALONEY + FRIENDS
GET STARTED

BALONEY
AND FRIENDS
GREG PIZZOLI

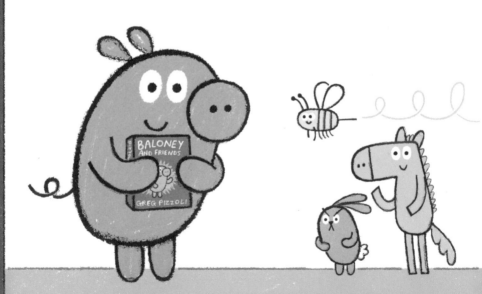

(AN INTRODUCTION OF SORTS)

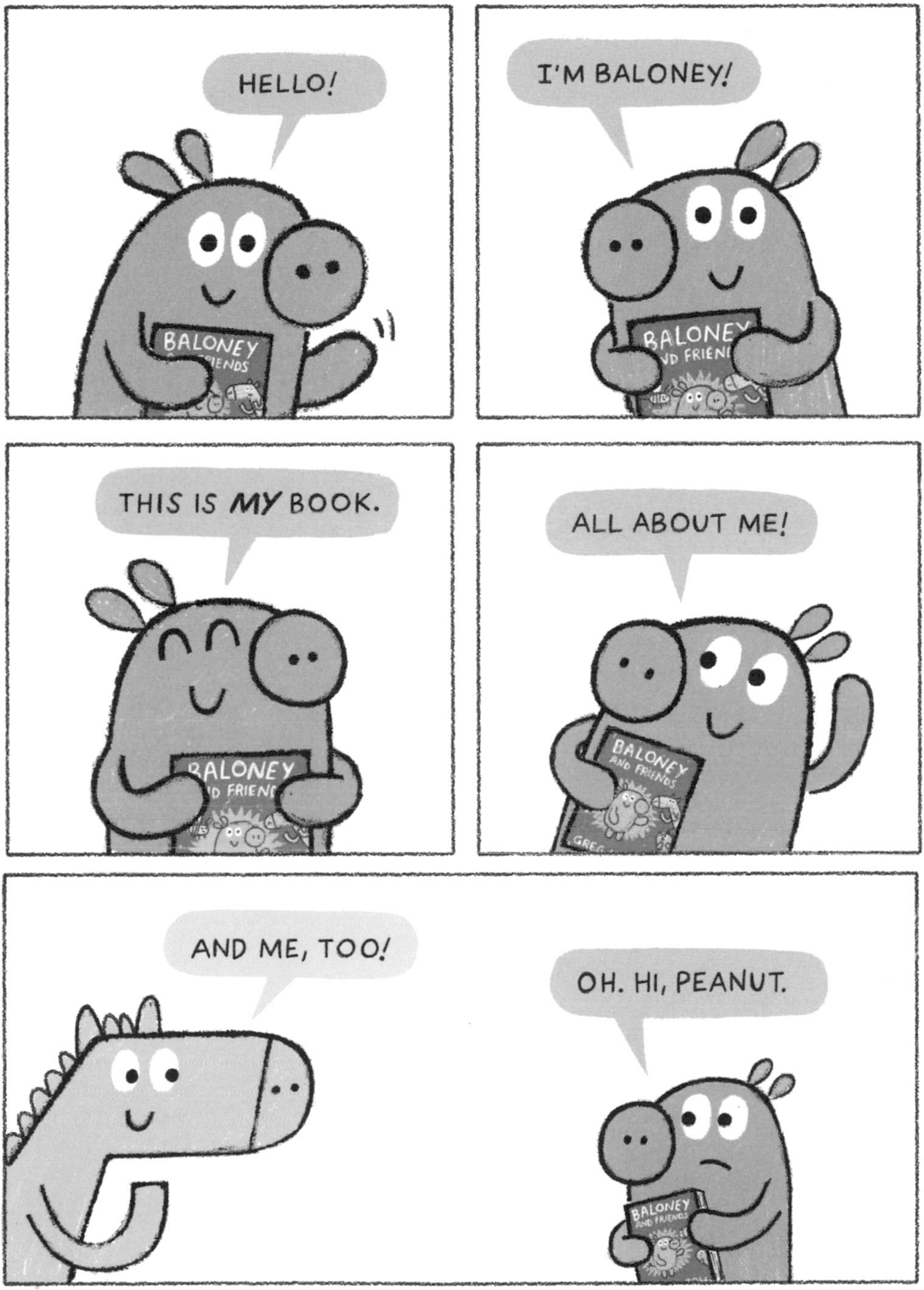
HELLO!
I'M BALONEY!
THIS IS *MY* BOOK.
ALL ABOUT ME!
AND ME, TOO!
OH. HI, PEANUT.

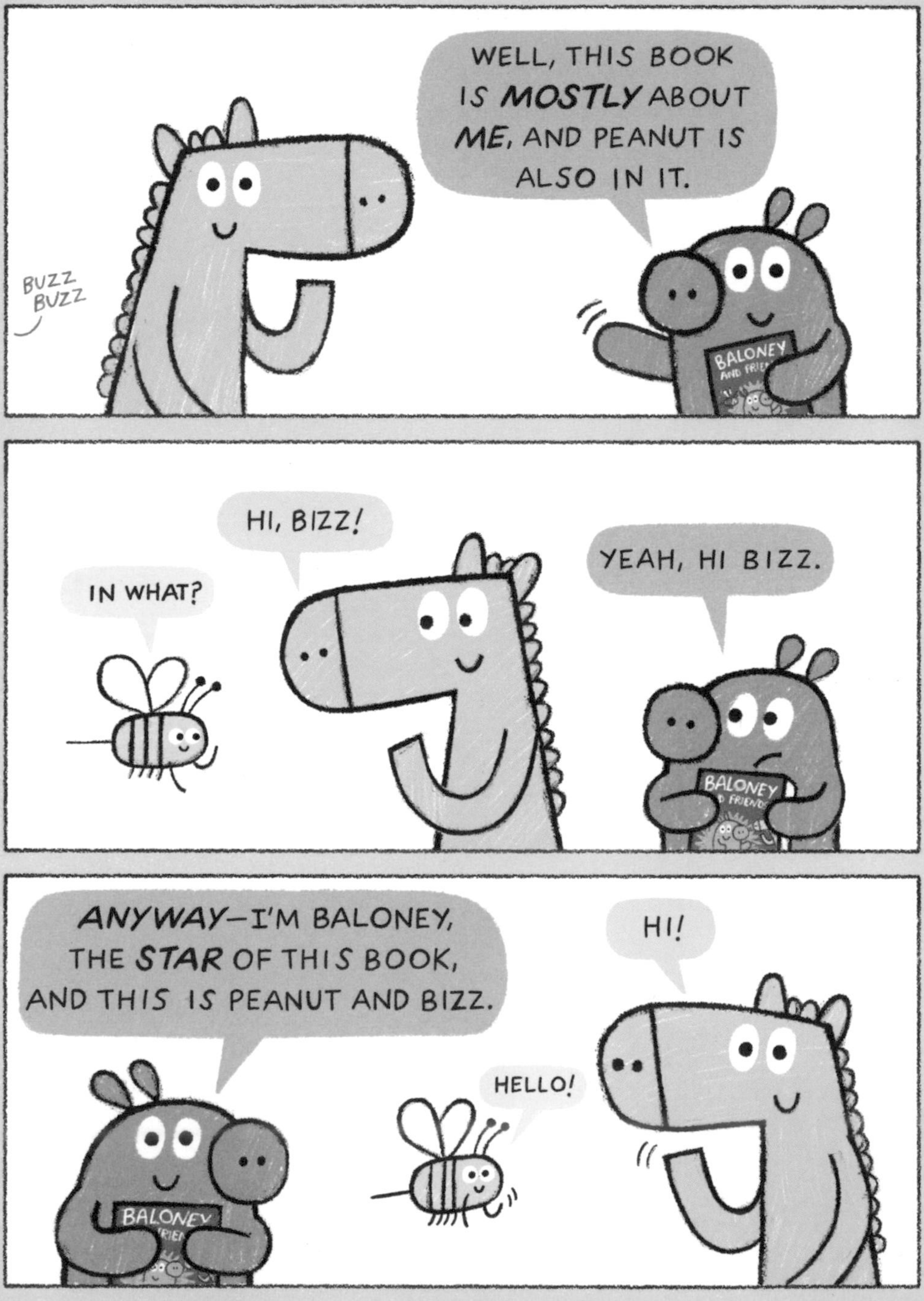
WELL, THIS BOOK IS MOSTLY ABOUT ME, AND PEANUT IS ALSO IN IT.
BUZZ BUZZ
BALONEY AND FRIENDS
IN WHAT?
HI, BIZZ!
YEAH, HI BIZZ.
BALONEY AND FRIENDS
ANYWAY—I'M BALONEY, THE STAR OF THIS BOOK, AND THIS IS PEANUT AND BIZZ.
HI!
HELLO!
BALONEY

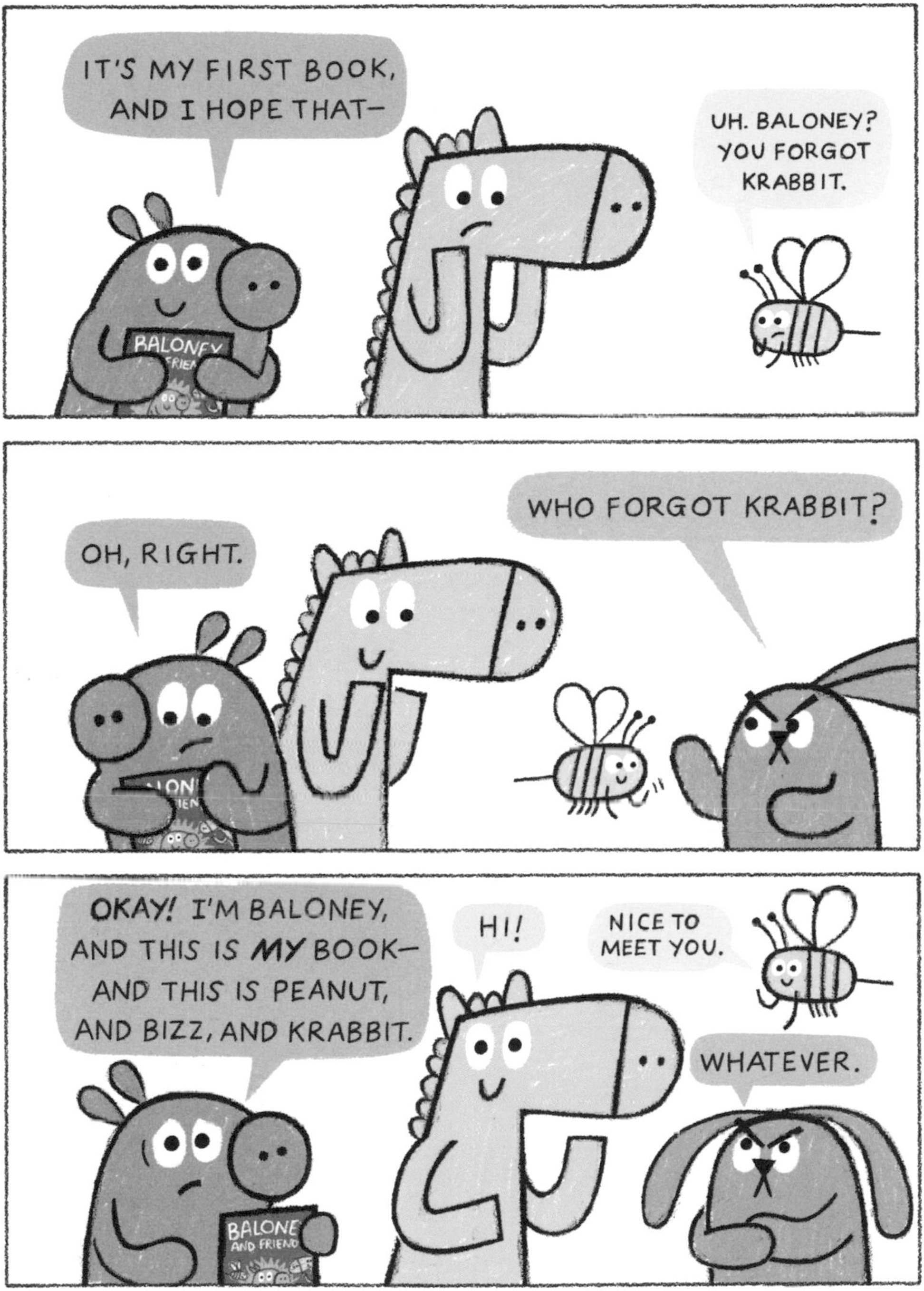
IT'S MY FIRST BOOK, AND I HOPE THAT—
UH. BALONEY? YOU FORGOT KRABBIT.
OH, RIGHT.
WHO FORGOT KRABBIT?
OKAY! I'M BALONEY, AND THIS IS MY BOOK— AND THIS IS PEANUT, AND BIZZ, AND KRABBIT.
HI!
NICE TO MEET YOU.
WHATEVER.

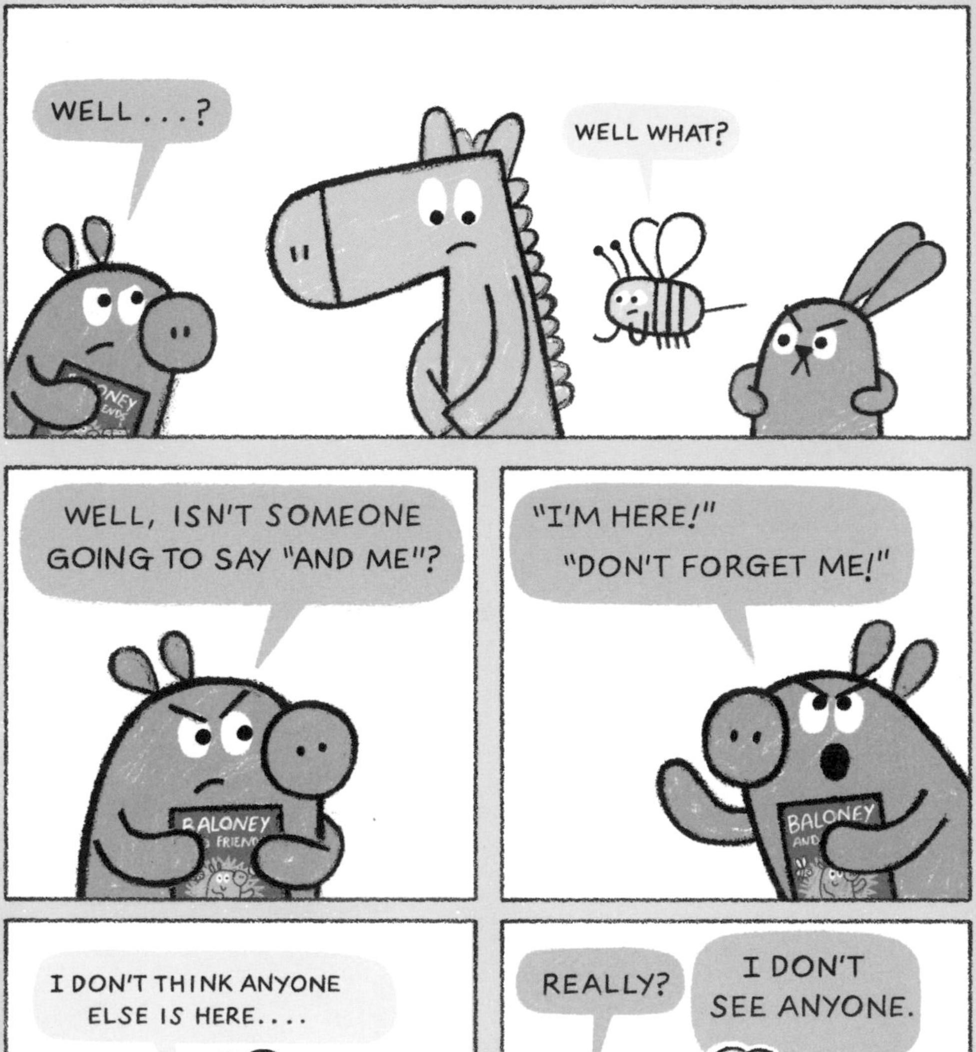
WELL . . . ?
WELL WHAT?
WELL, ISN'T SOMEONE GOING TO SAY "AND ME"?
"I'M HERE!" "DON'T FORGET ME!"
I DON'T THINK ANYONE ELSE IS HERE. . . .
REALLY?
I DON'T SEE ANYONE.

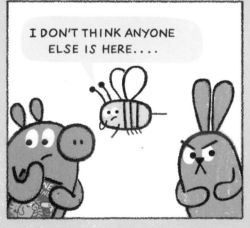

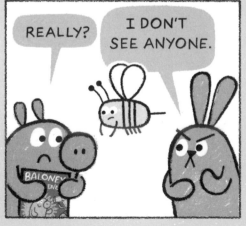

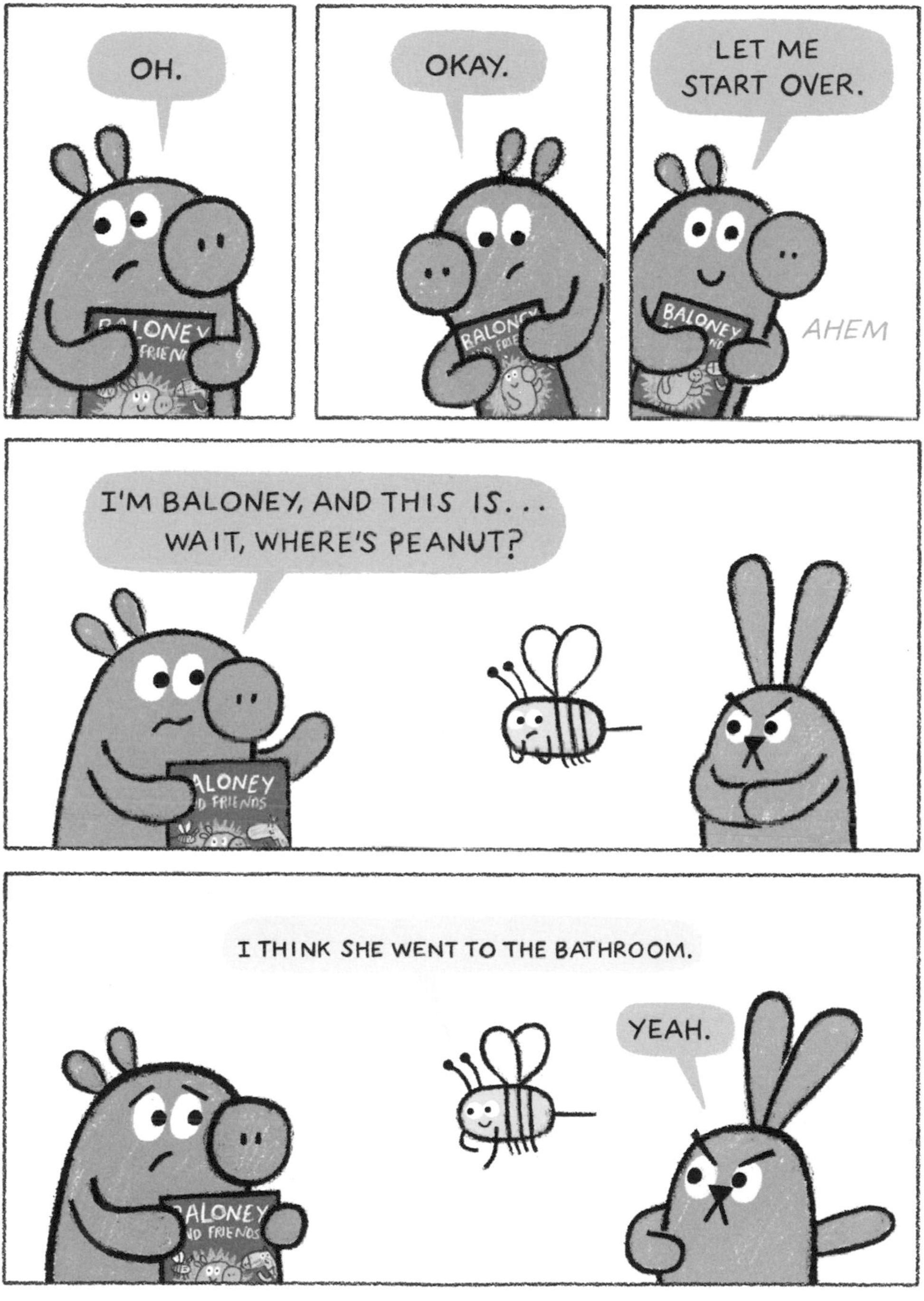
OH.
OKAY.
LET ME START OVER.
AHEM
I'M BALONEY, AND THIS IS... WAIT, WHERE'S PEANUT?
I THINK SHE WENT TO THE BATHROOM.
YEAH.

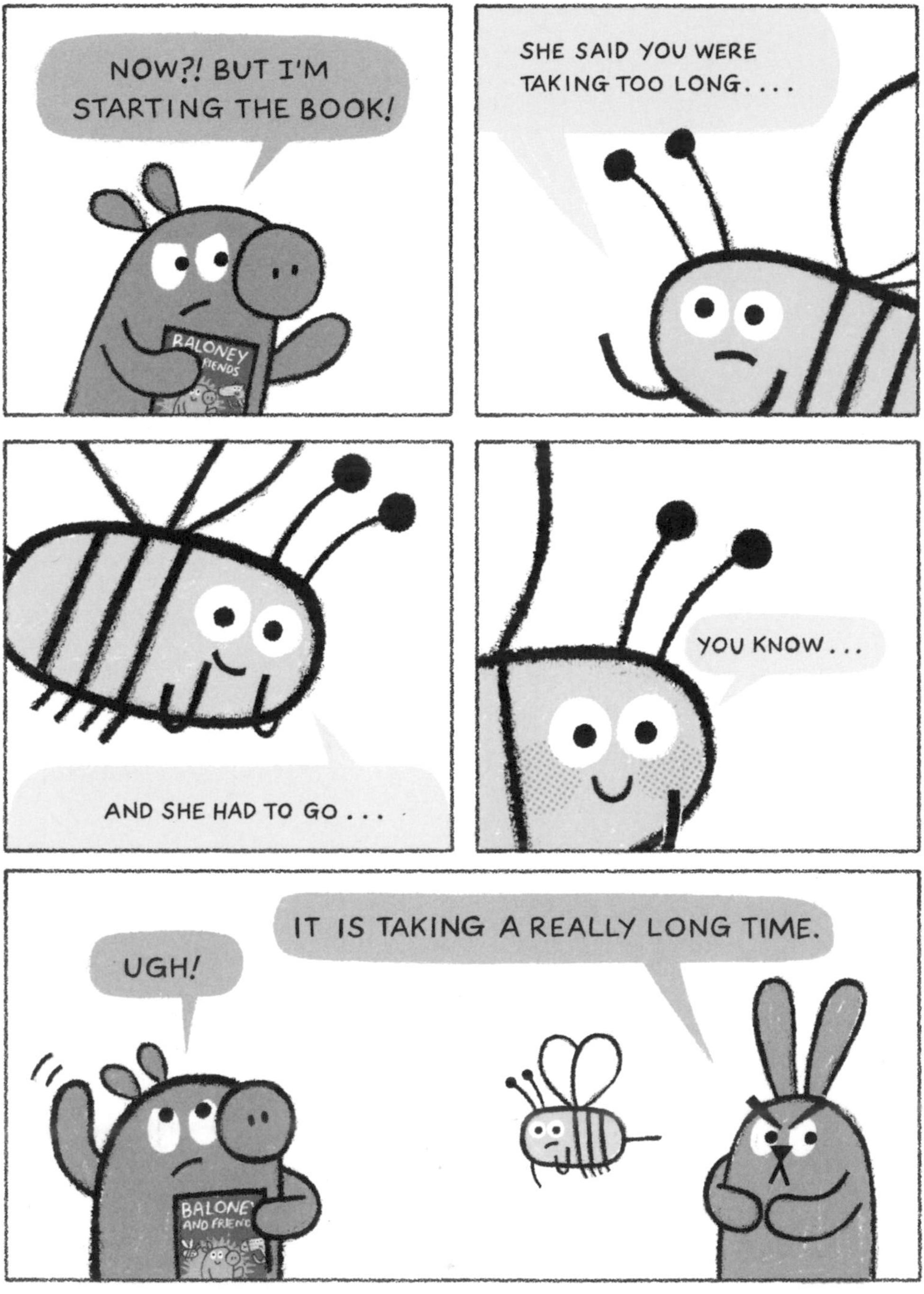
NOW?! BUT I'M STARTING THE BOOK!
BALONEY FRIENDS
SHE SAID YOU WERE TAKING TOO LONG....
AND SHE HAD TO GO...
YOU KNOW...
UGH!
IT IS TAKING A REALLY LONG TIME.
BALONEY AND FRIENDS

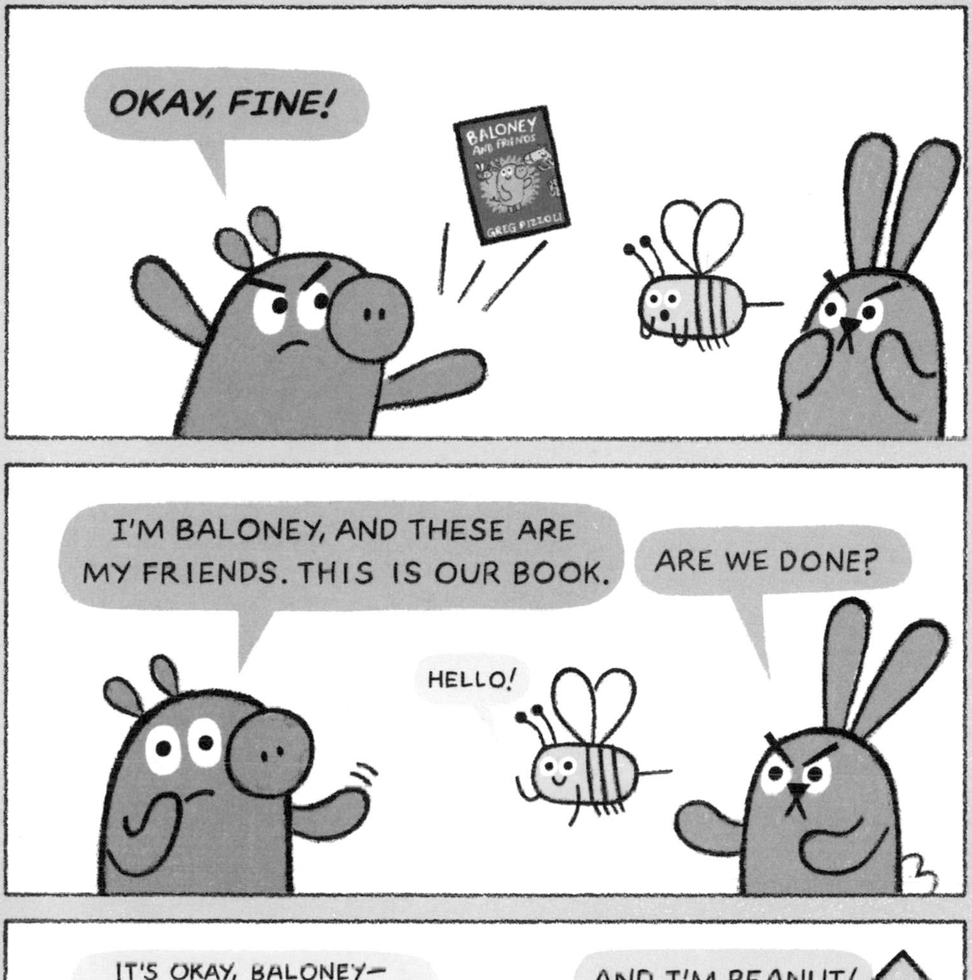
OKAY, FINE!
BALONEY AND FRIENDS
GREG PIZZOLI
I'M BALONEY, AND THESE ARE MY FRIENDS. THIS IS OUR BOOK.
HELLO!
ARE WE DONE?
IT'S OKAY, BALONEY— I THOUGHT YOU DID GREAT.
WHATEVER.
AND I'M PEANUT!
END

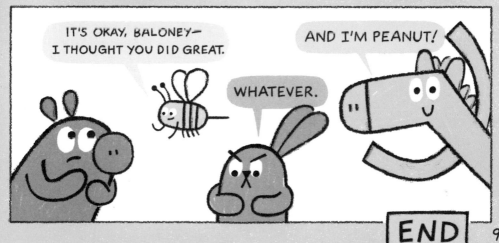

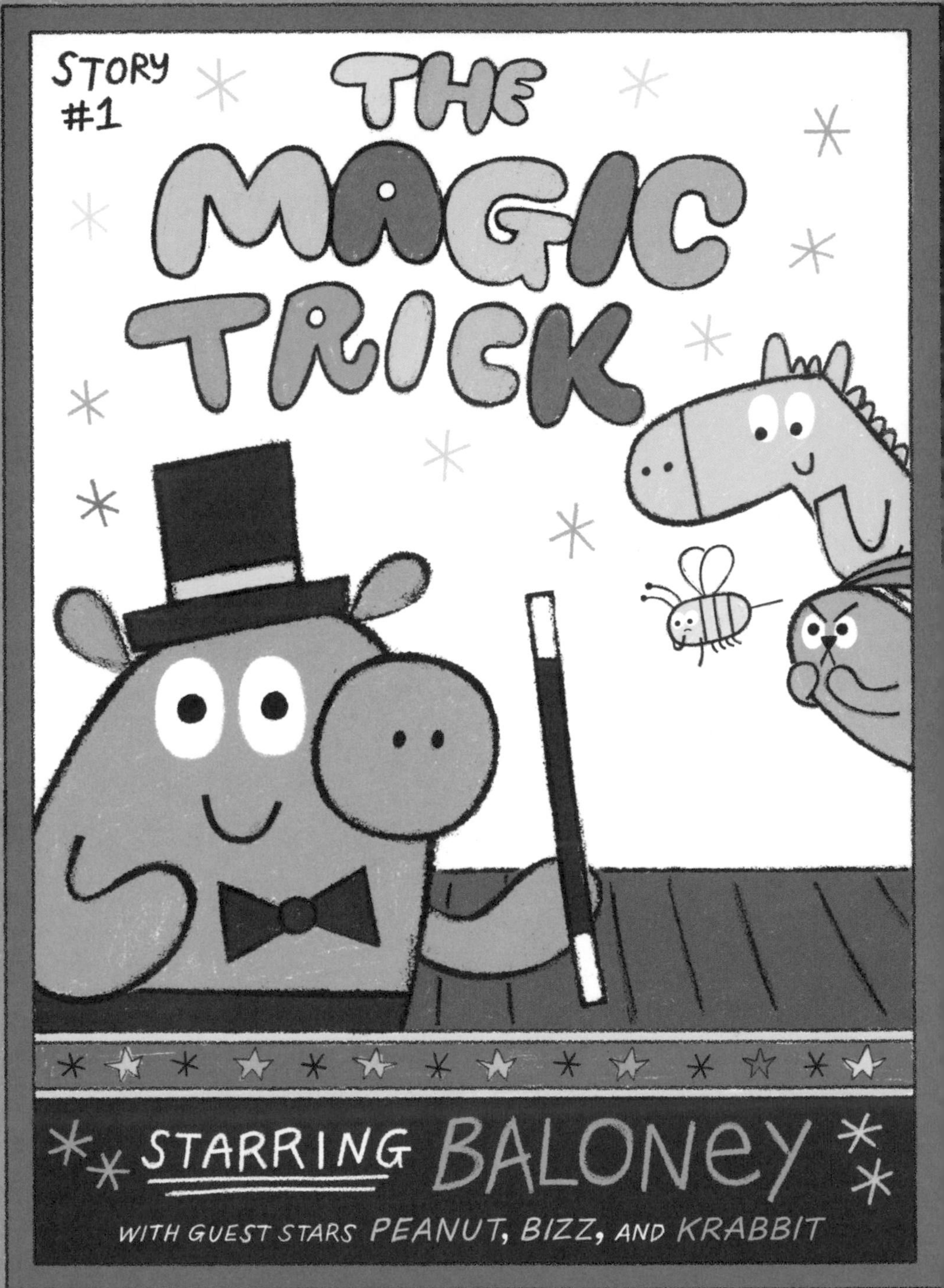
STORY #1
THE MAGIC TRICK
STARRING BALONEY
WITH GUEST STARS PEANUT, BIZZ, AND KRABBIT

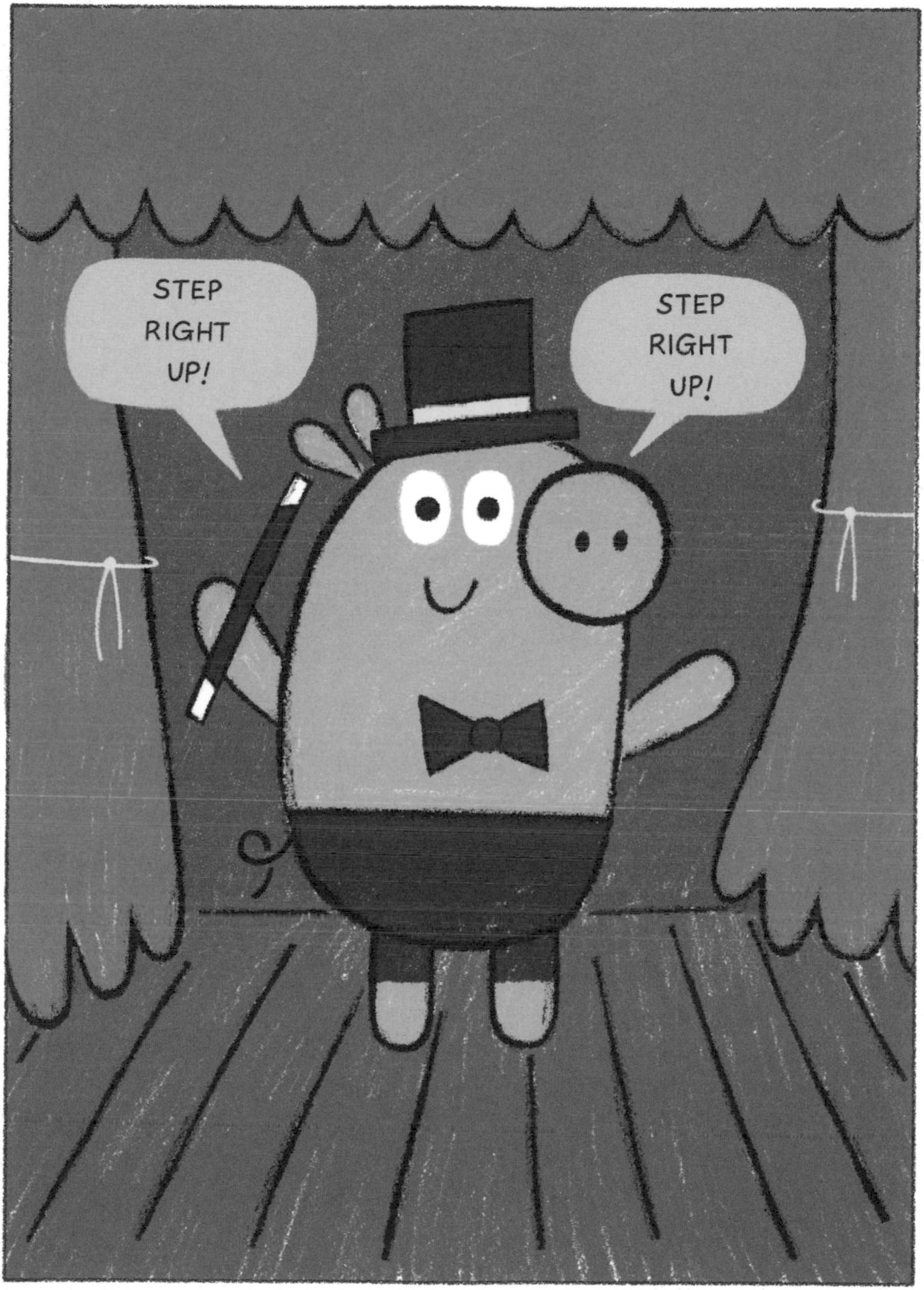
STEP RIGHT UP!
STEP RIGHT UP!

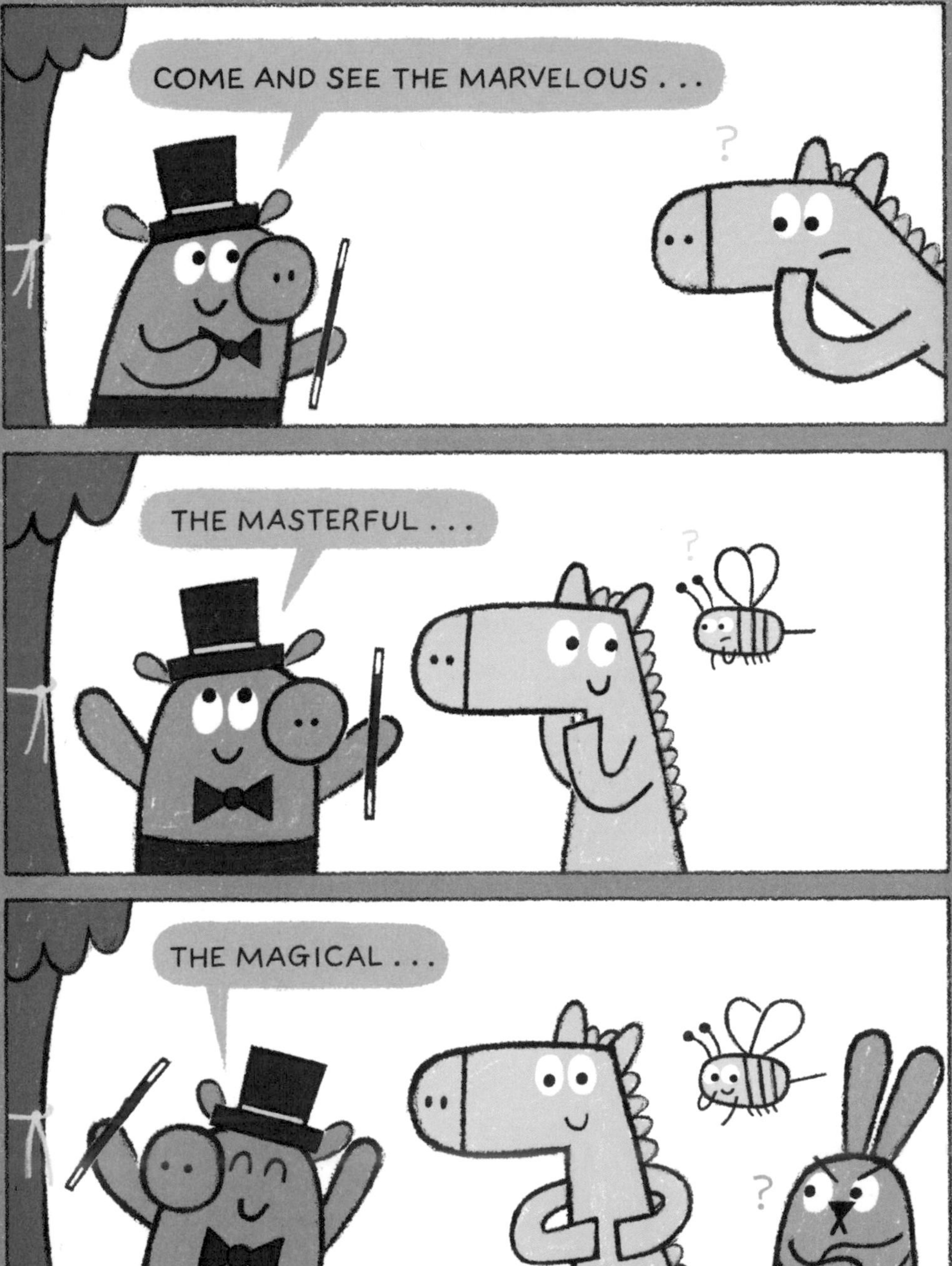
COME AND SEE THE MARVELOUS . . .
?
THE MASTERFUL . . .
?
THE MAGICAL . . .
?

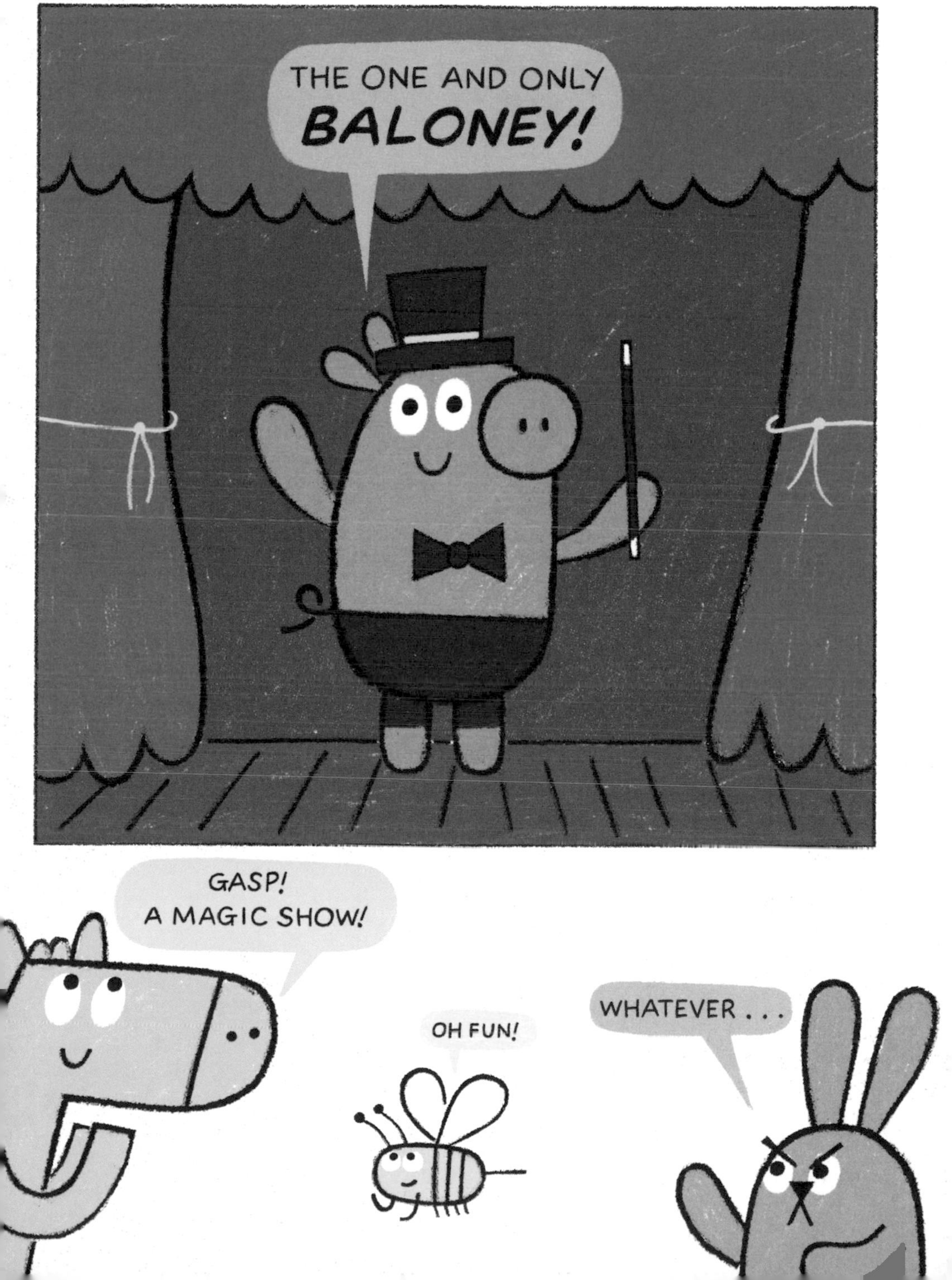
THE ONE AND ONLY
BALONEY!
GASP!
A MAGIC SHOW!
OH FUN!
WHATEVER . . .

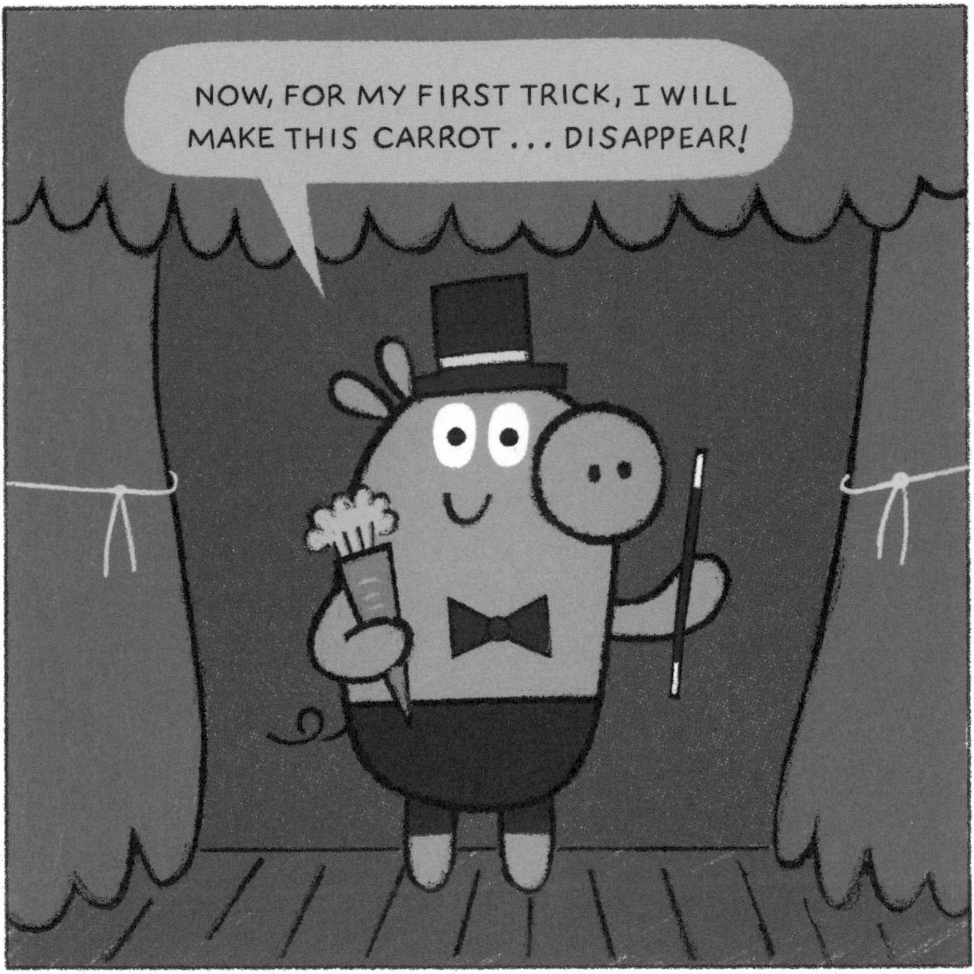
NOW, FOR MY FIRST TRICK, I WILL MAKE THIS CARROT . . . DISAPPEAR!

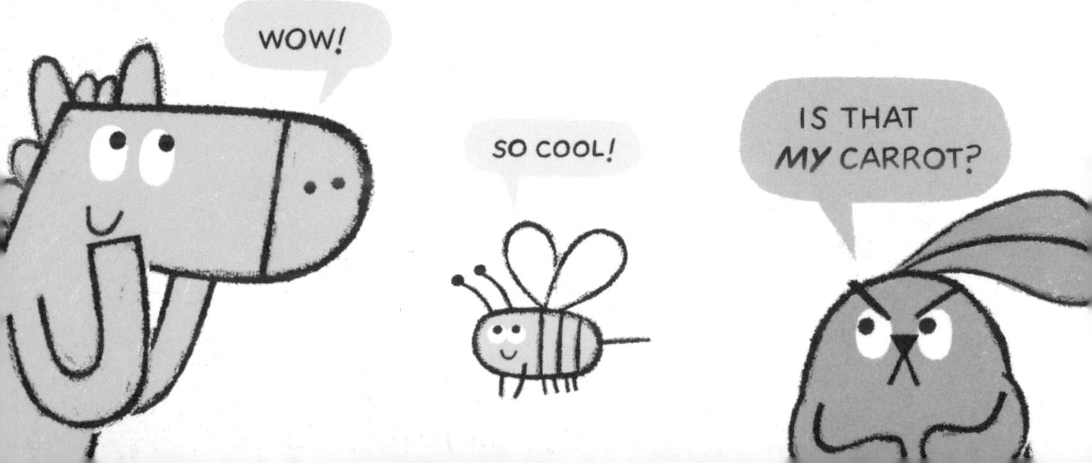
WOW!
SO COOL!
IS THAT *MY* CARROT?

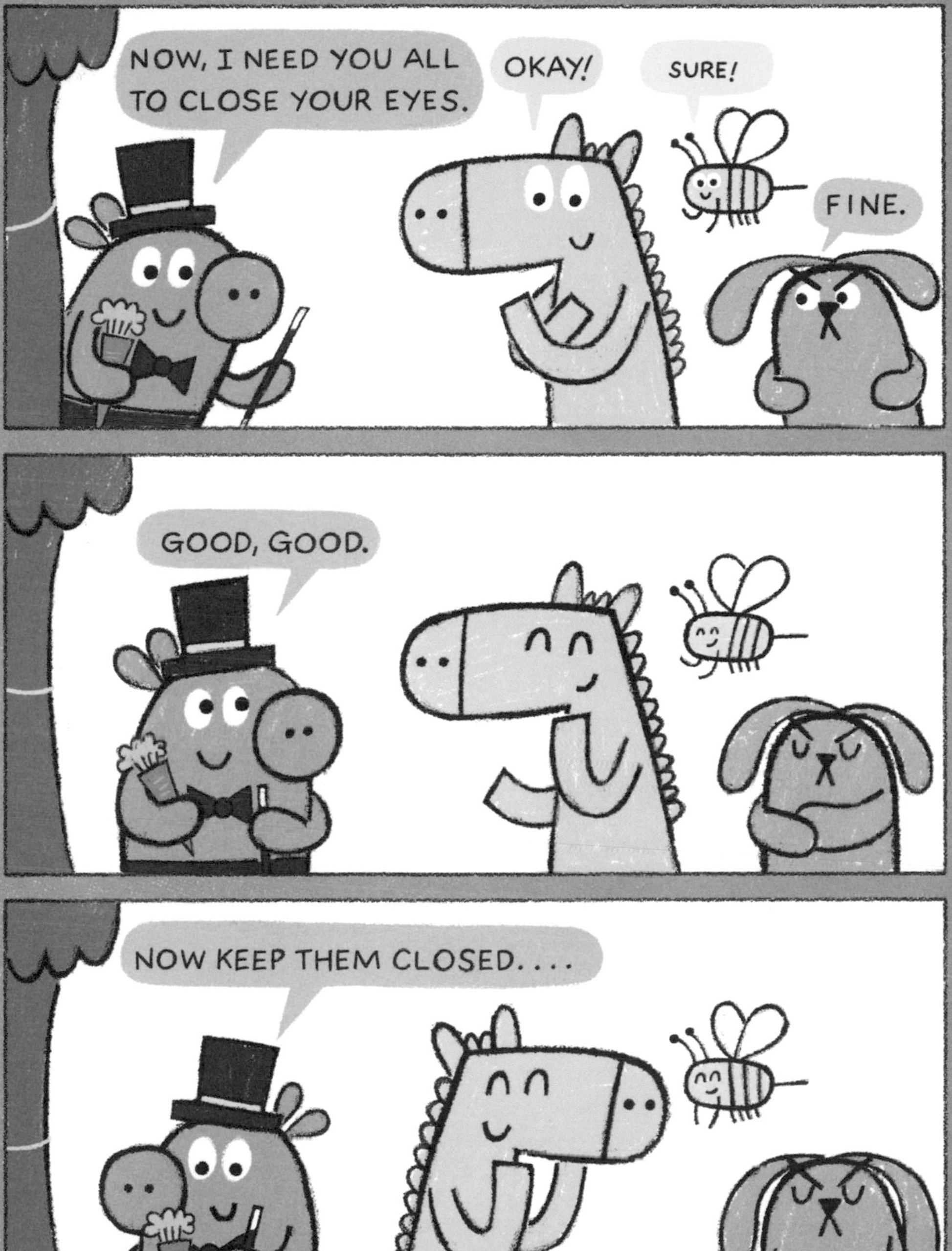
NOW, I NEED YOU ALL TO CLOSE YOUR EYES.
OKAY!
SURE!
FINE.
GOOD, GOOD.
NOW KEEP THEM CLOSED. . . .

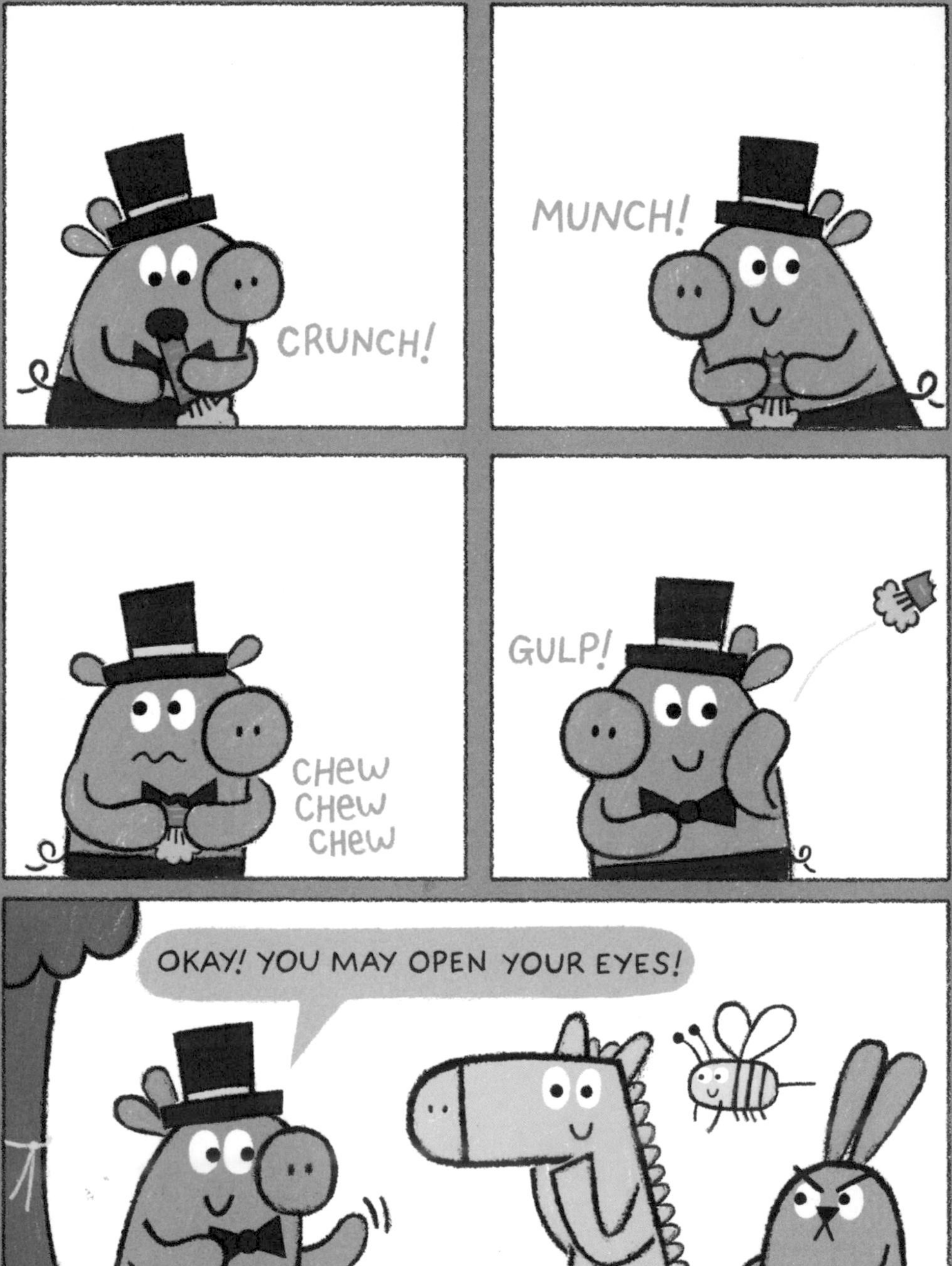
CRUNCH!
MUNCH!
CHEW
CHEW
CHEW
GULP!
OKAY! YOU MAY OPEN YOUR EYES!

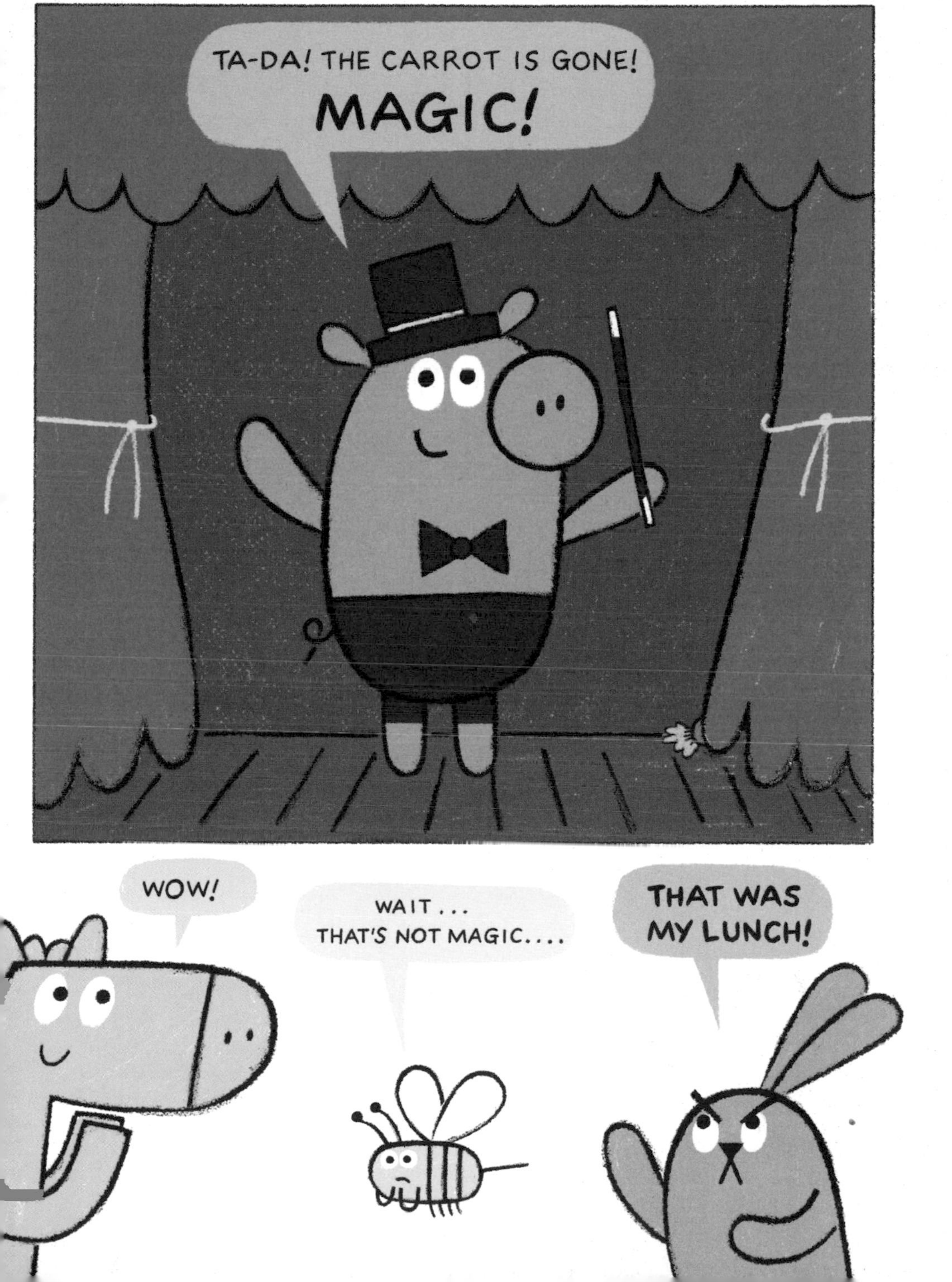
TA-DA! THE CARROT IS GONE!
MAGIC!
WOW!
WAIT . . .
THAT'S NOT MAGIC. . . .
THAT WAS MY LUNCH!

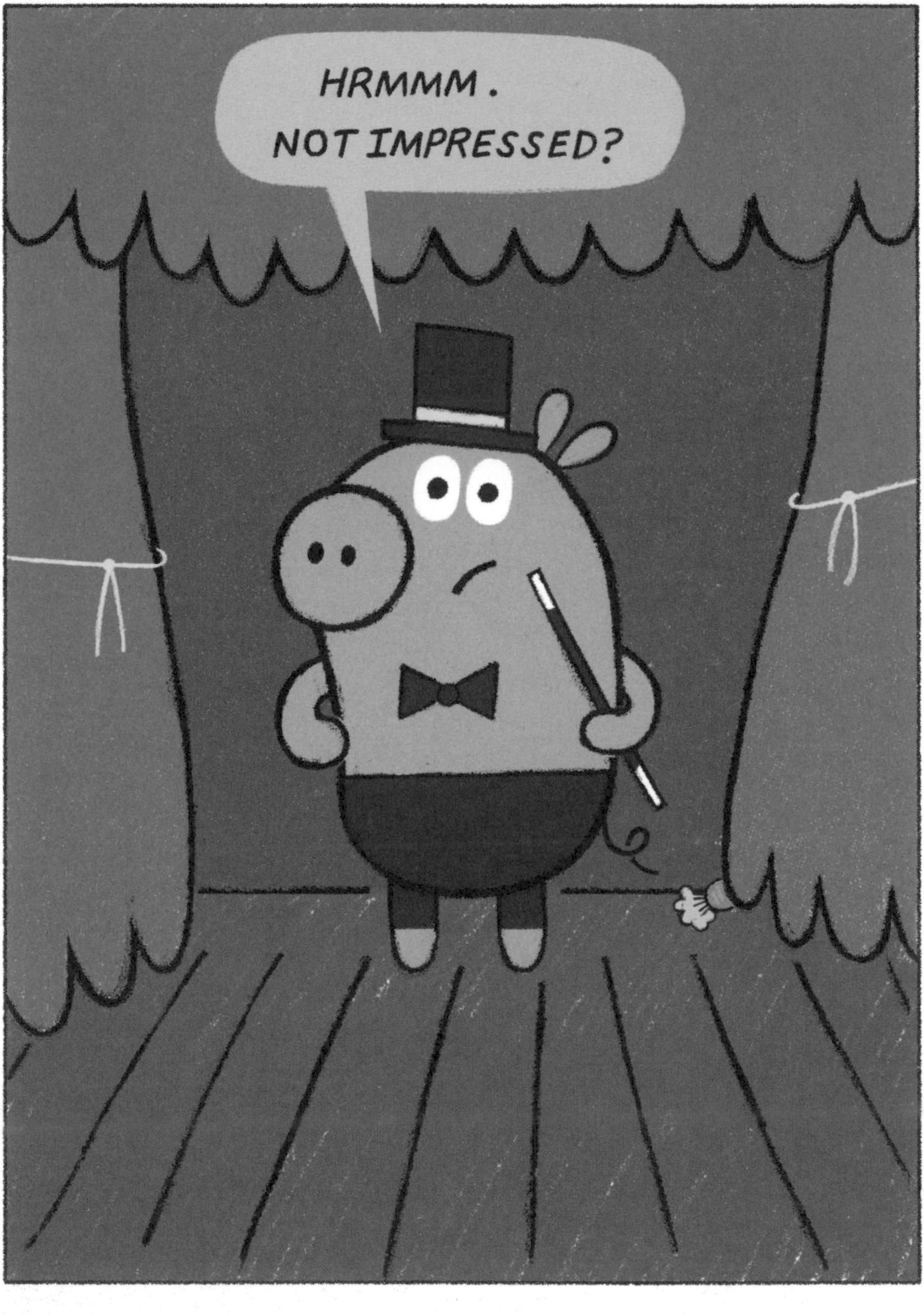
HRMMM.
NOT IMPRESSED?

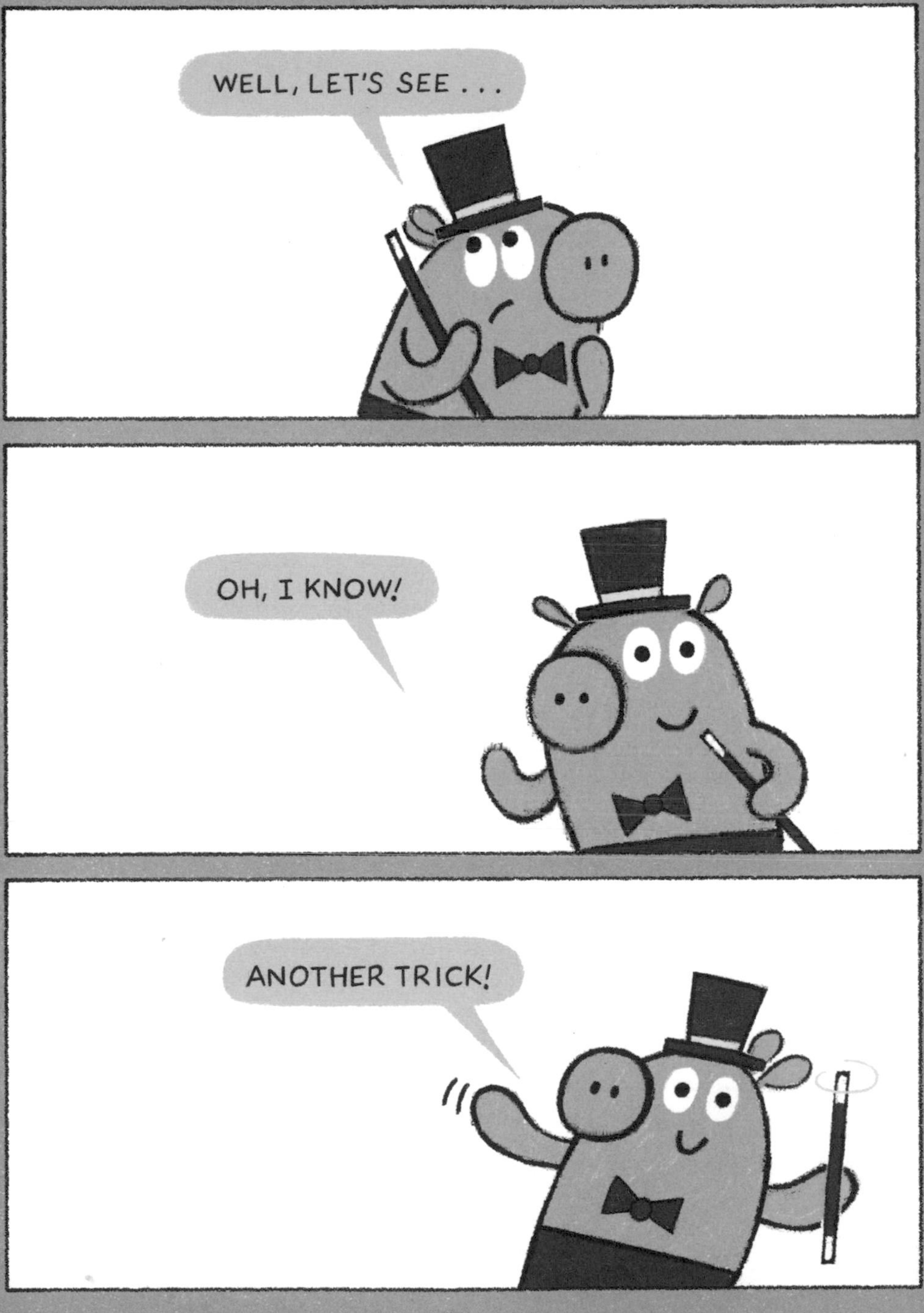
WELL, LET'S SEE . . .
OH, I KNOW!
ANOTHER TRICK!

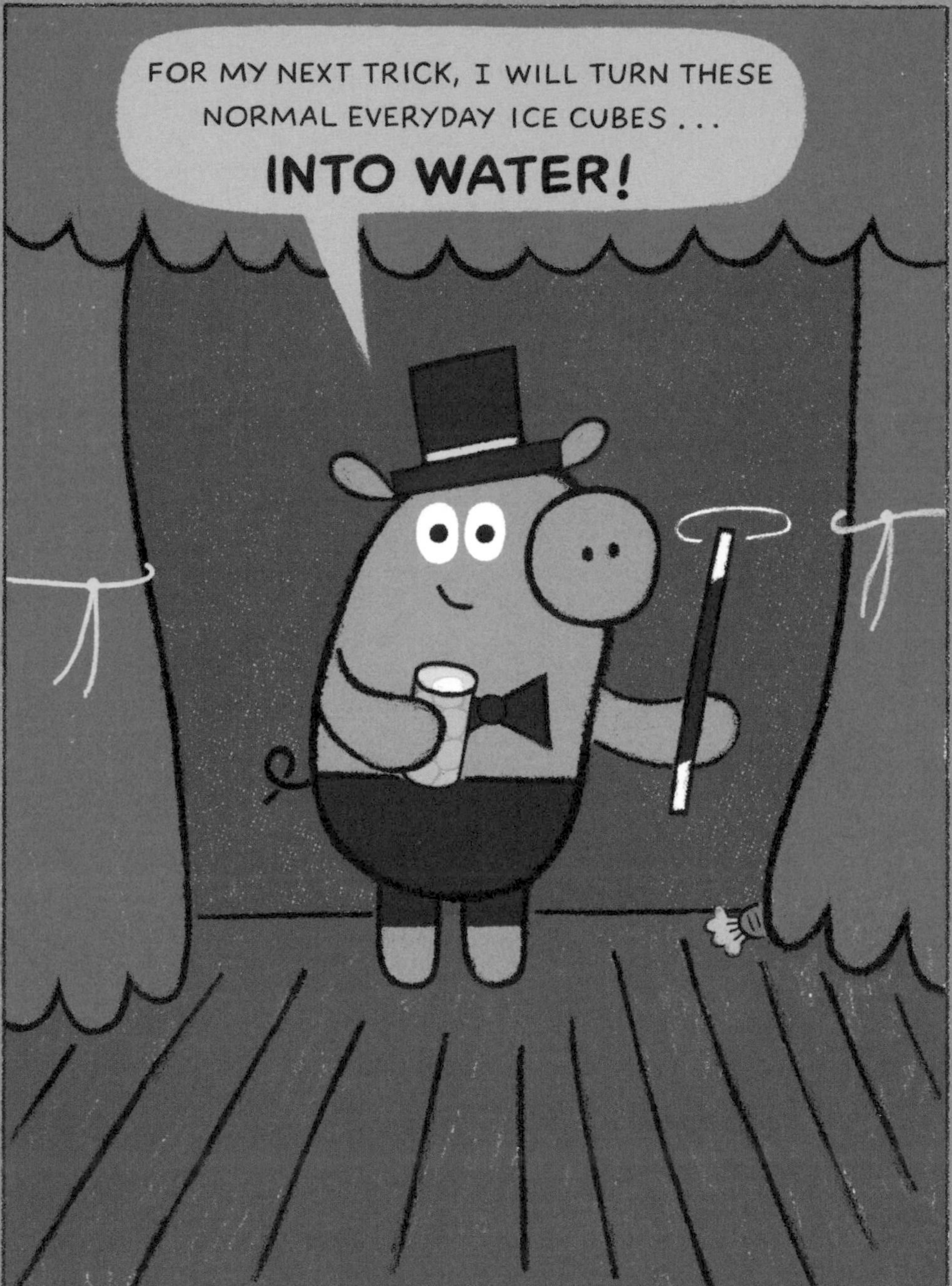
FOR MY NEXT TRICK, I WILL TURN THESE NORMAL EVERYDAY ICE CUBES . . .
INTO WATER!

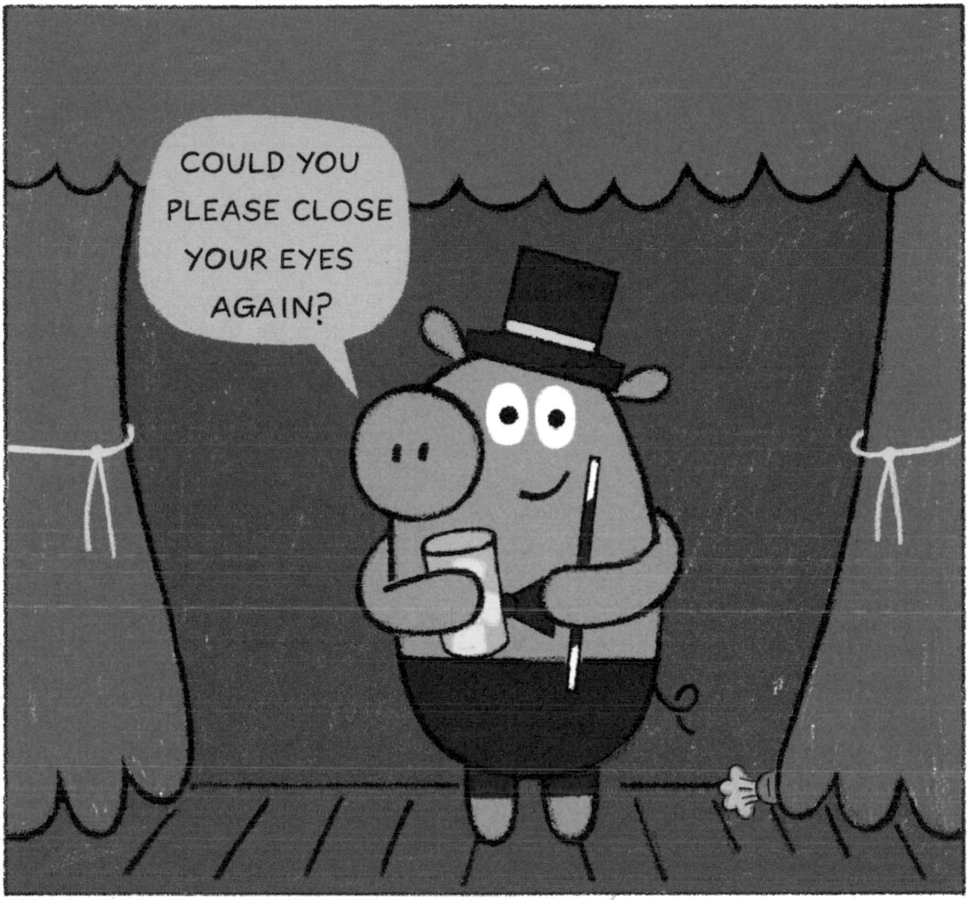
COULD YOU PLEASE CLOSE YOUR EYES AGAIN?

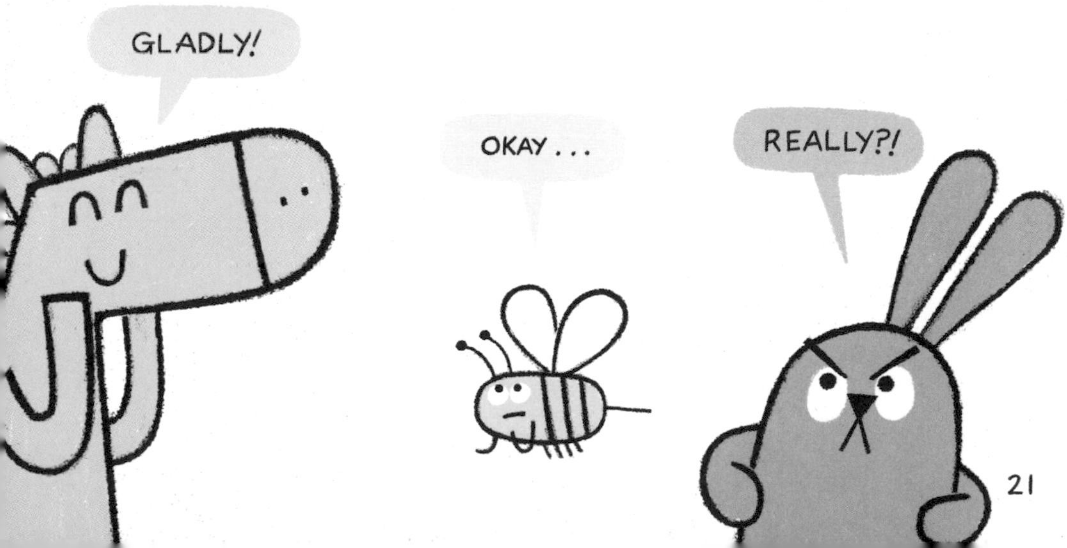
GLADLY!
OKAY . . .
REALLY?!

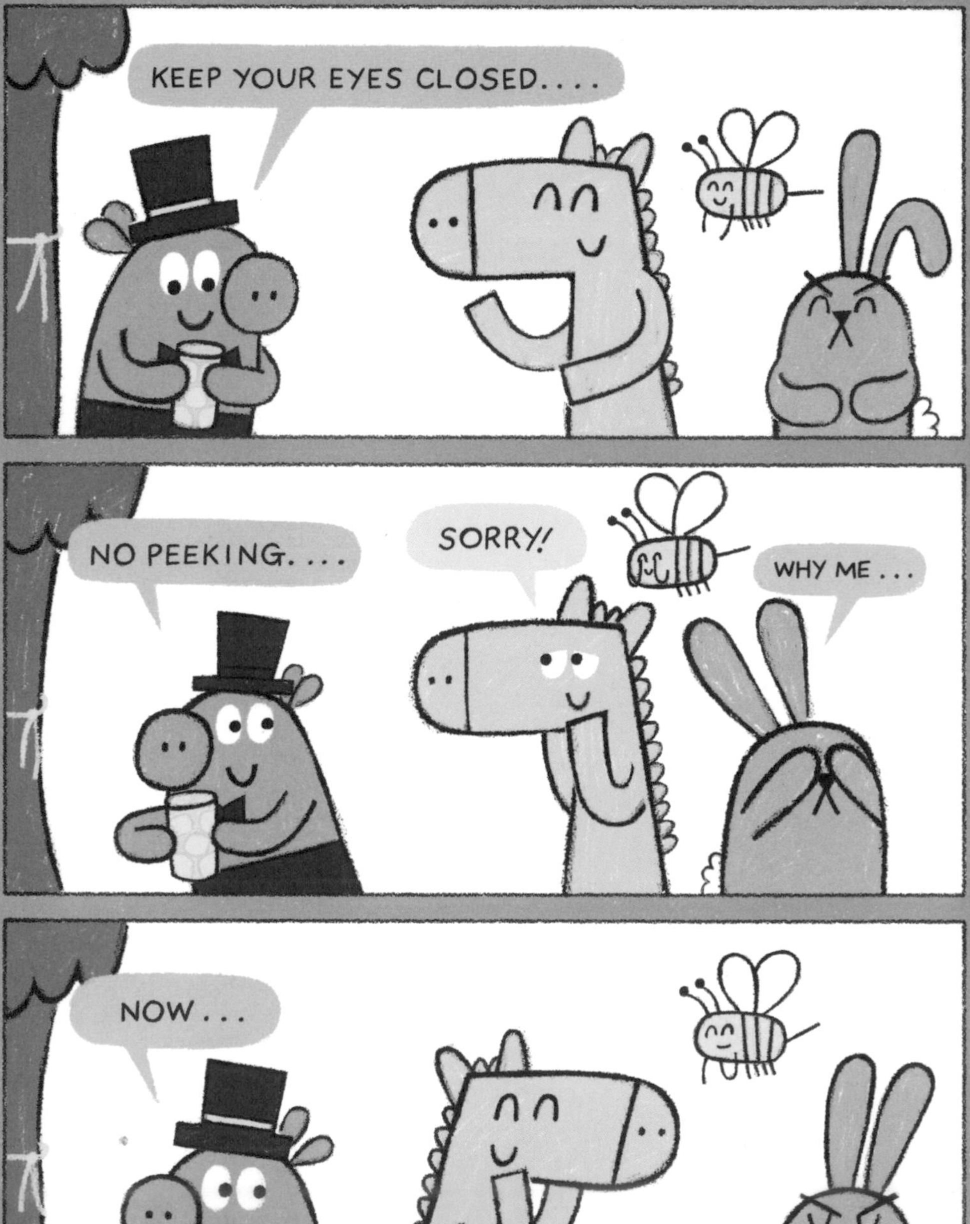
KEEP YOUR EYES CLOSED....
NO PEEKING....
SORRY!
WHY ME...
NOW...

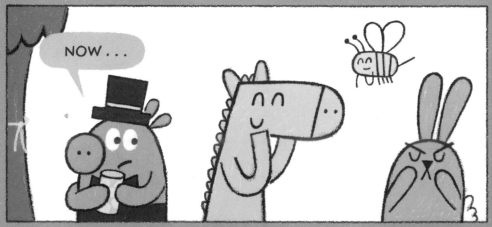

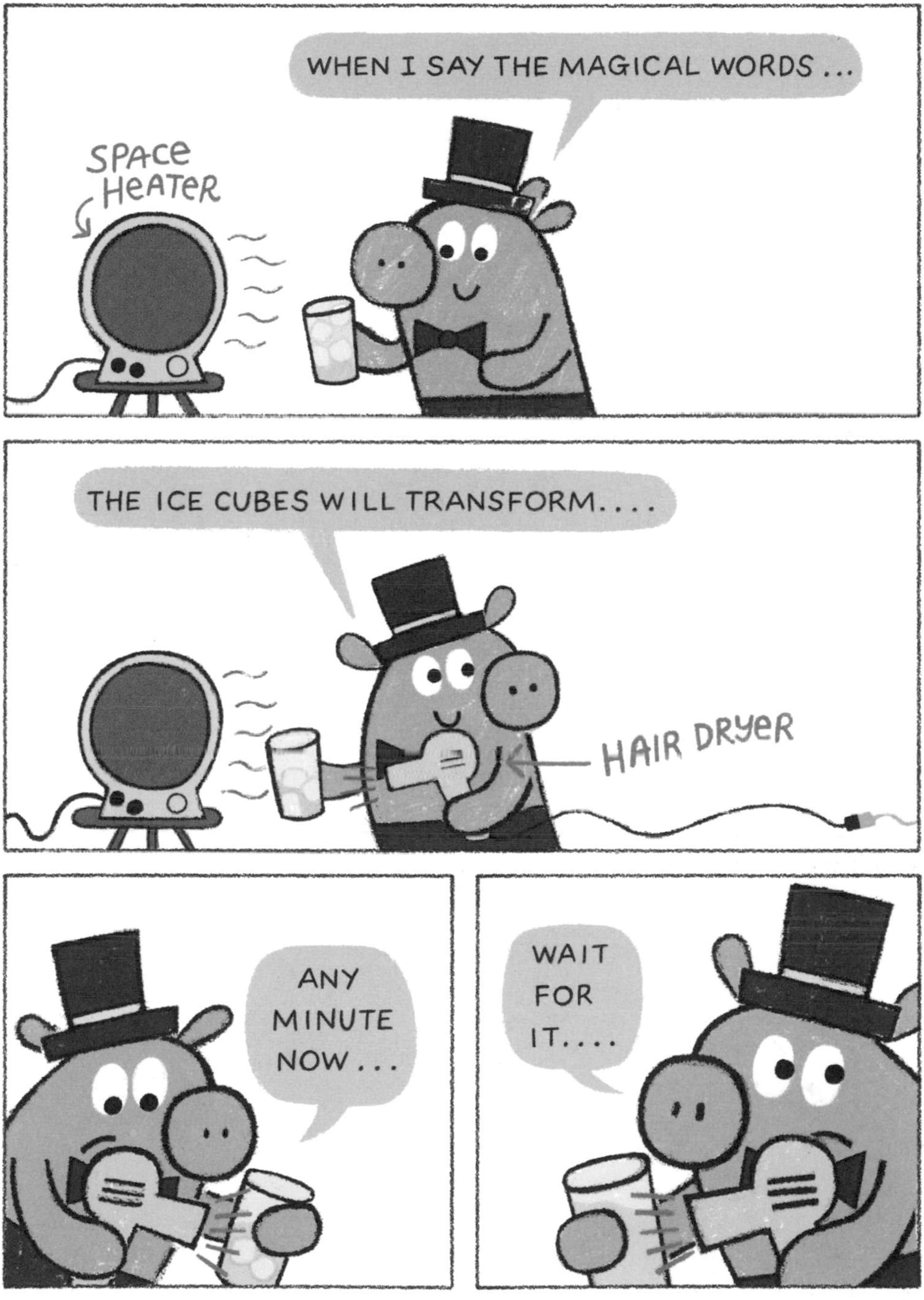
WHEN I SAY THE MAGICAL WORDS...
SPACE HEATER
THE ICE CUBES WILL TRANSFORM....
HAIR DRYER
ANY MINUTE NOW...
WAIT FOR IT....

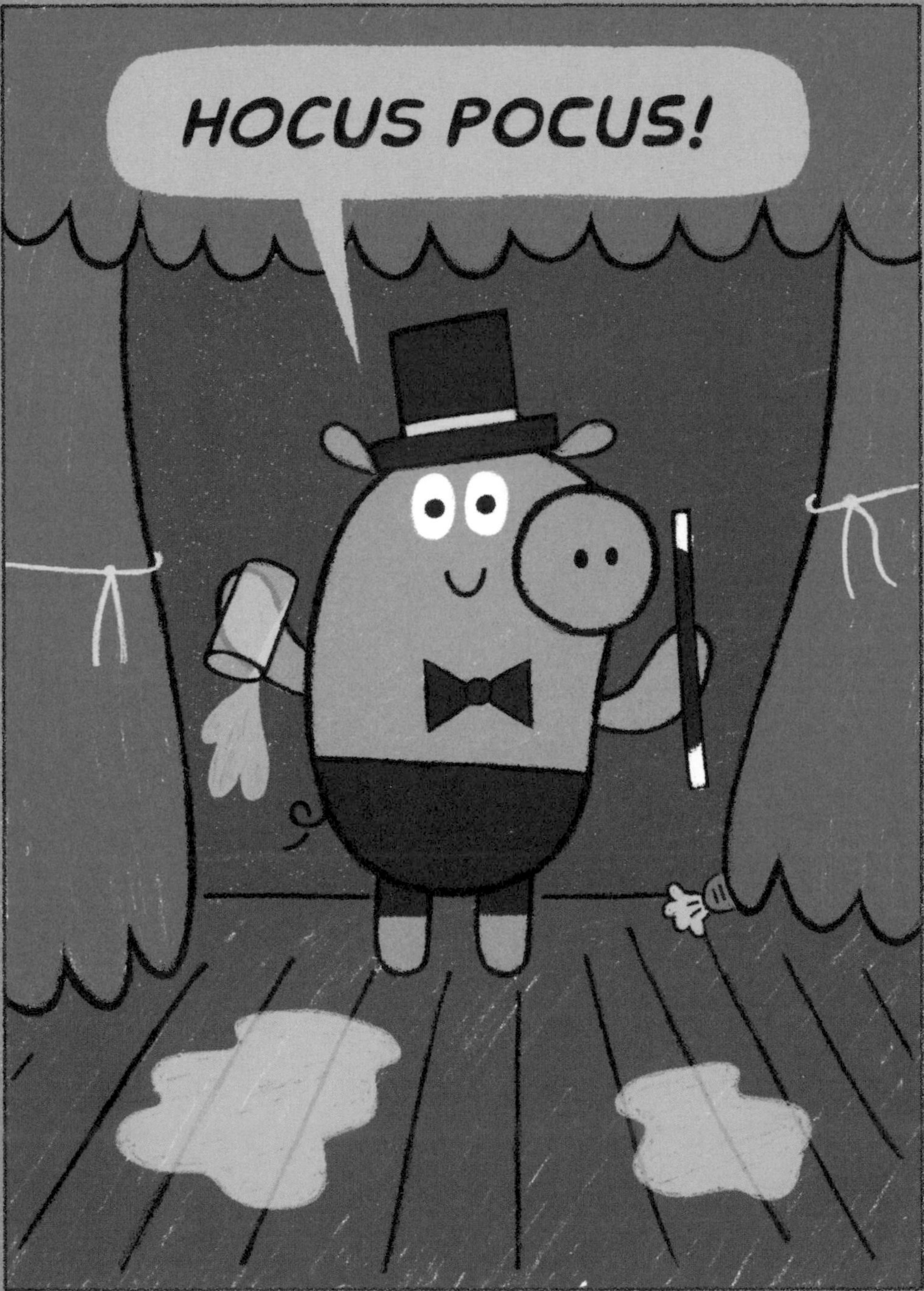
HOCUS POCUS!

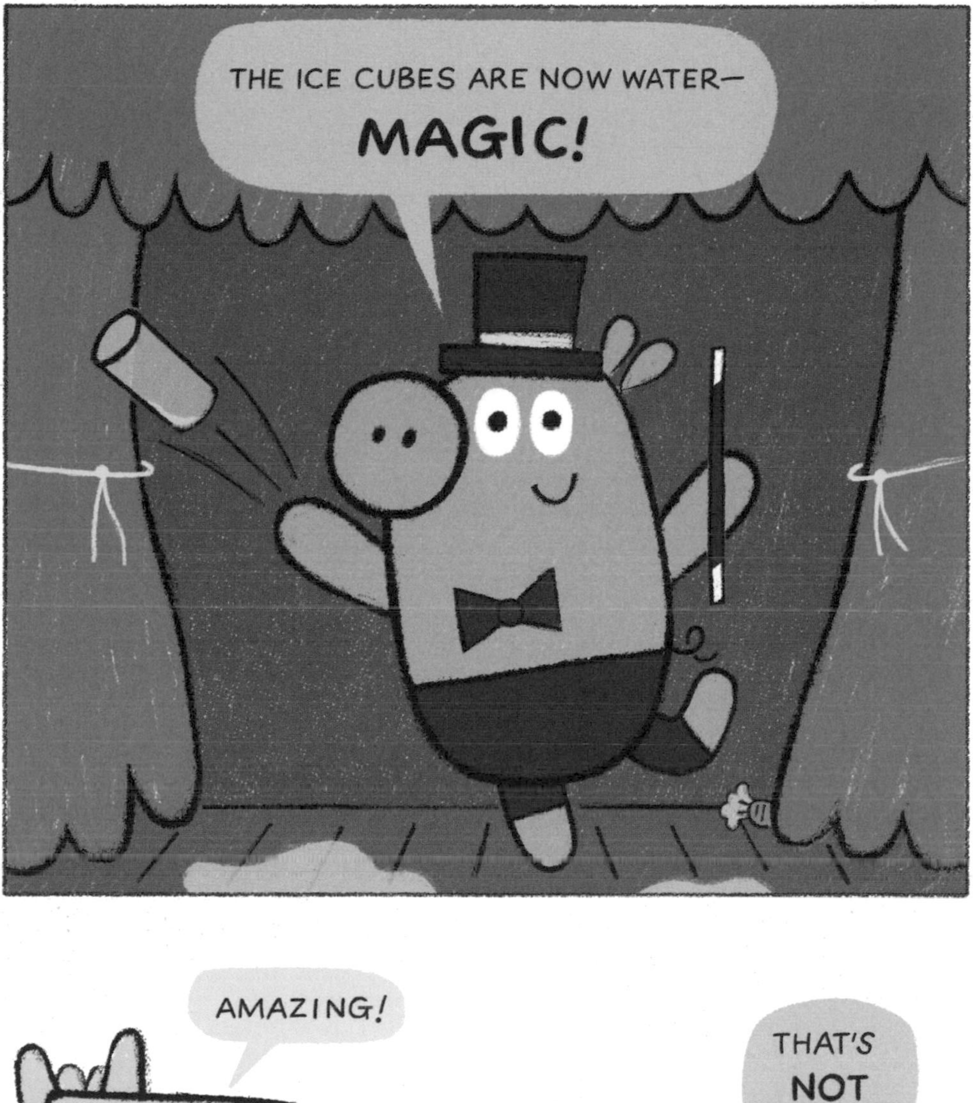
THE ICE CUBES ARE NOW WATER—
MAGIC!

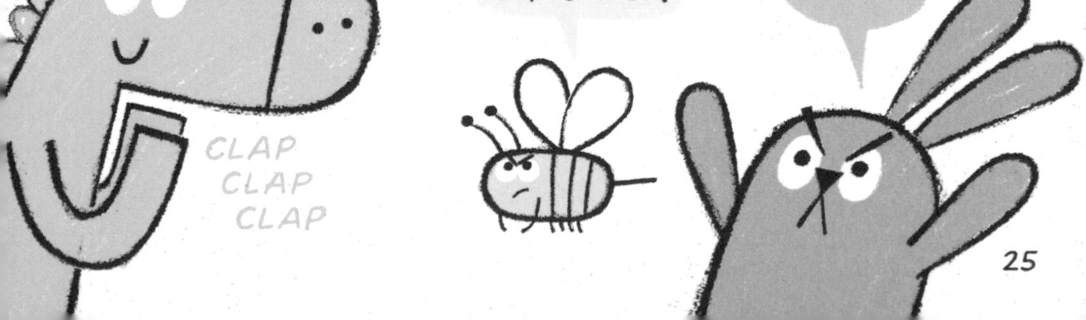
AMAZING!
CLAP
CLAP
CLAP
OH, COME ON!
THAT'S NOT MAGIC!

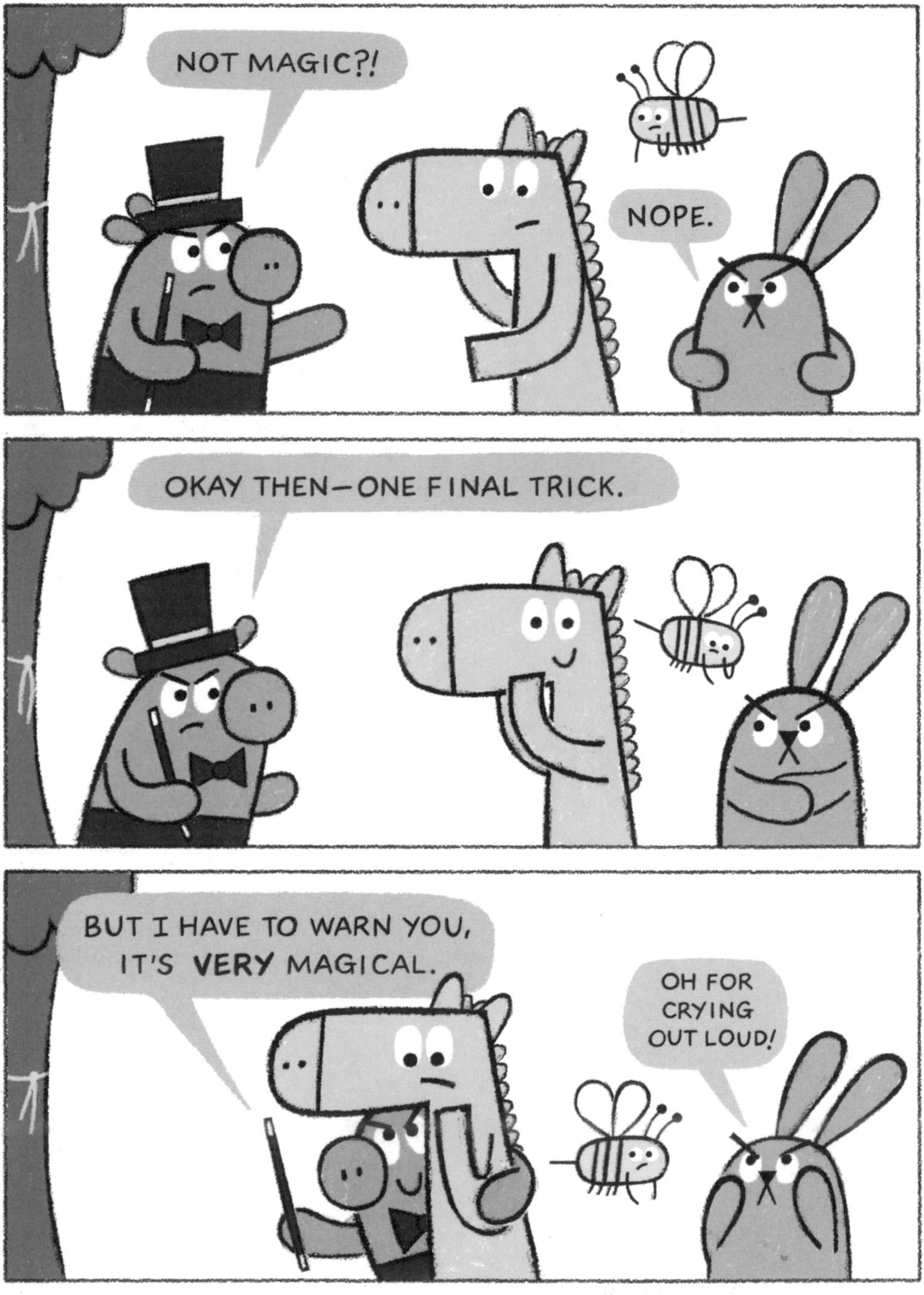
NOT MAGIC?!
NOPE.
OKAY THEN—ONE FINAL TRICK.
BUT I HAVE TO WARN YOU, IT'S **VERY** MAGICAL.
OH FOR CRYING OUT LOUD!

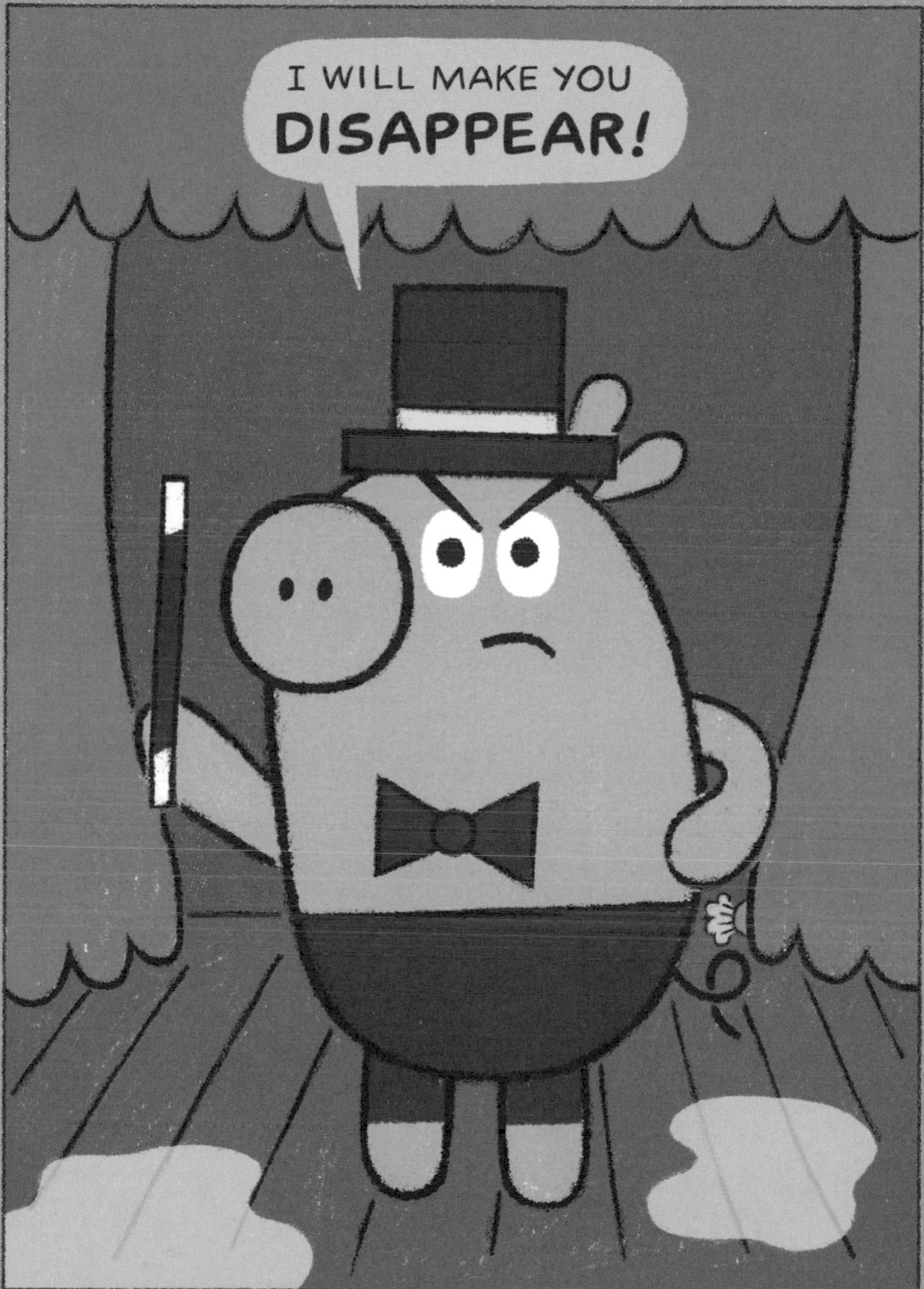
I WILL MAKE YOU DISAPPEAR!

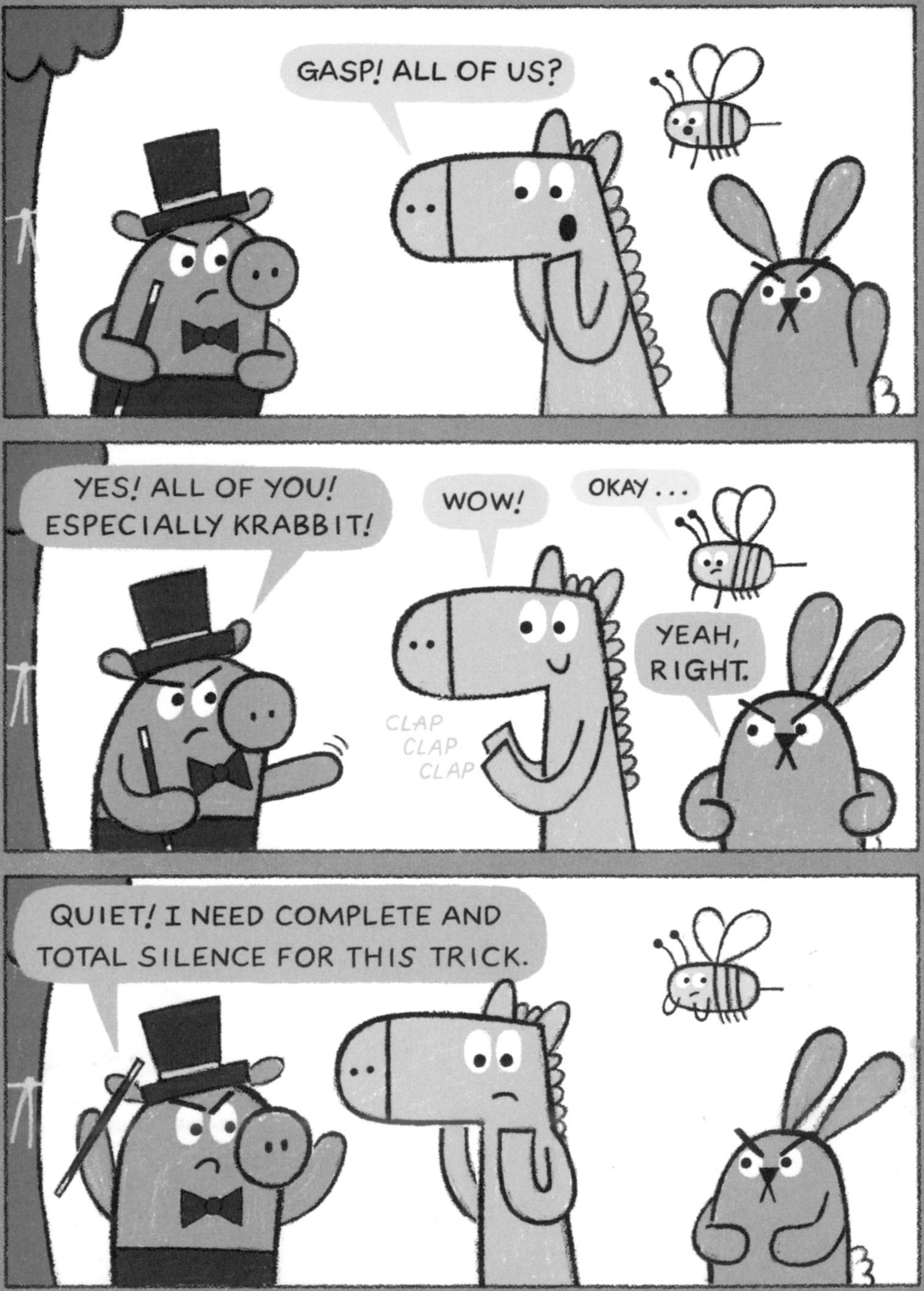
GASP! ALL OF US?
YES! ALL OF YOU! ESPECIALLY KRABBIT!
WOW!
OKAY . . .
YEAH, RIGHT.
CLAP CLAP CLAP
QUIET! I NEED COMPLETE AND TOTAL SILENCE FOR THIS TRICK.

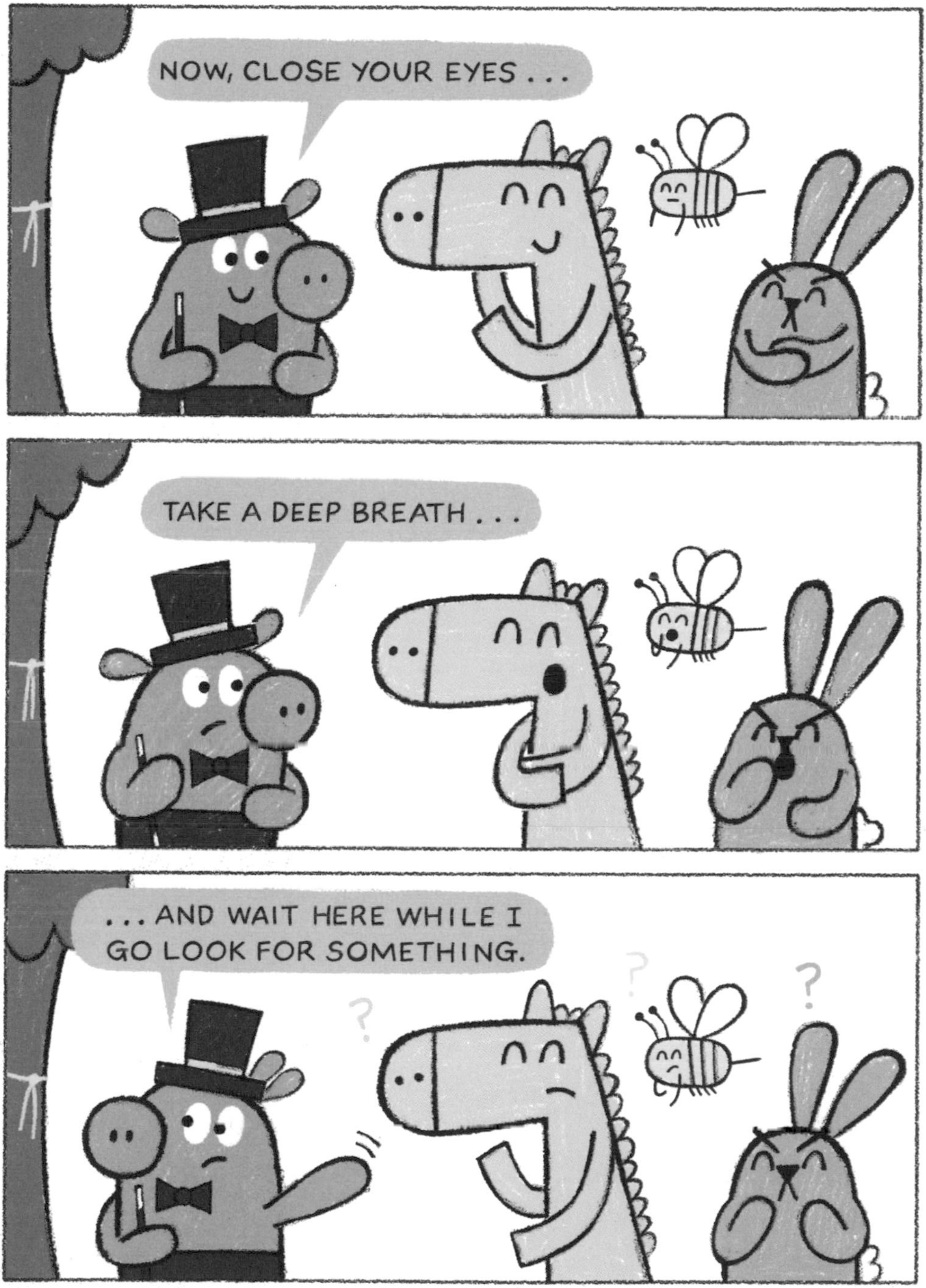
NOW, CLOSE YOUR EYES . . .
TAKE A DEEP BREATH . . .
. . . AND WAIT HERE WHILE I GO LOOK FOR SOMETHING.
?
?
?

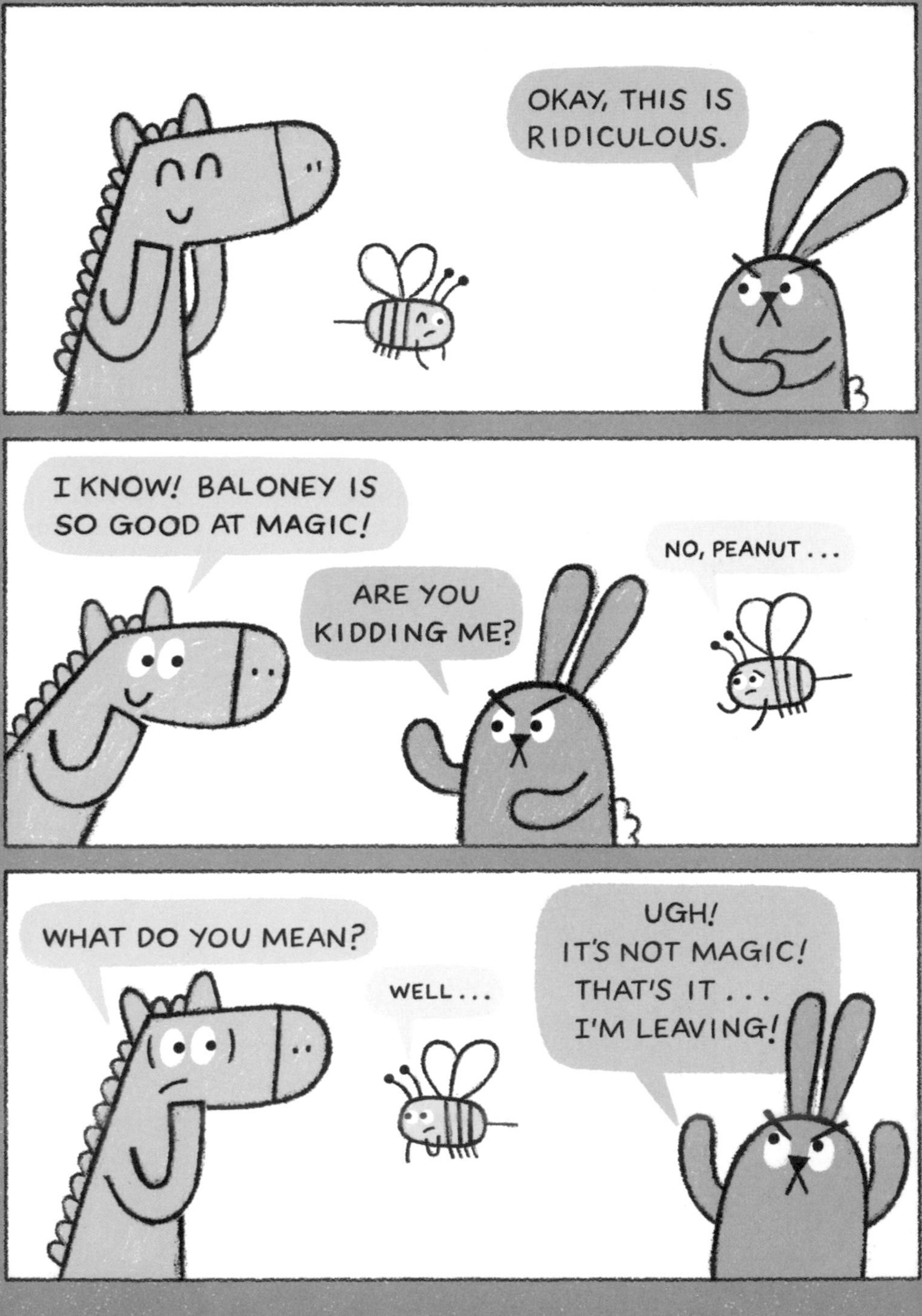
OKAY, THIS IS RIDICULOUS.
I KNOW! BALONEY IS SO GOOD AT MAGIC!
ARE YOU KIDDING ME?
NO, PEANUT . . .
WHAT DO YOU MEAN?
WELL . . .
UGH! IT'S NOT MAGIC! THAT'S IT . . . I'M LEAVING!

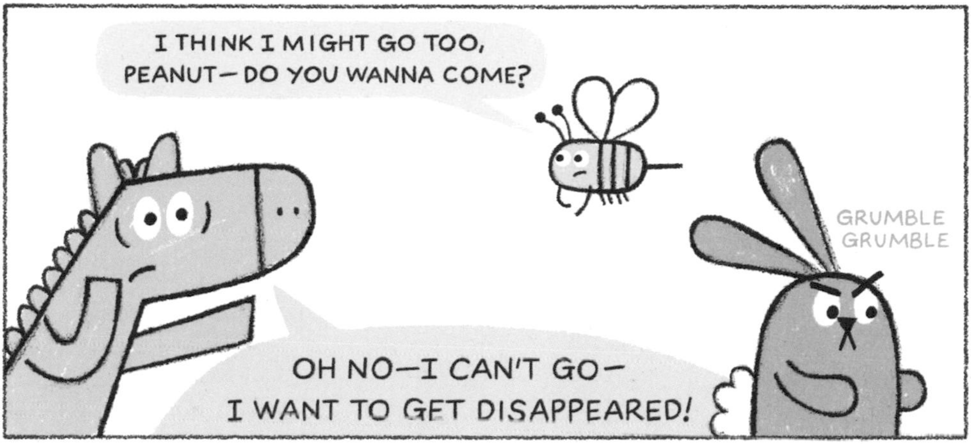
I THINK I MIGHT GO TOO, PEANUT— DO YOU WANNA COME?
GRUMBLE GRUMBLE
OH NO—I CAN'T GO— I WANT TO GET DISAPPEARED!

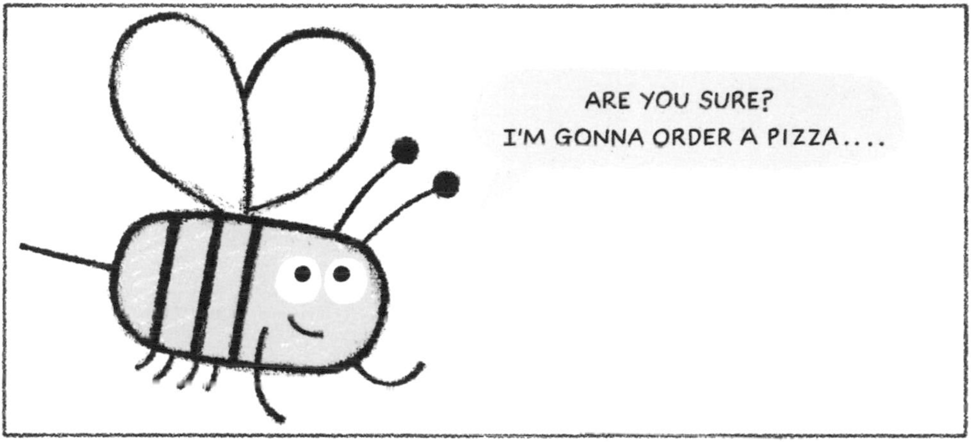
ARE YOU SURE? I'M GONNA ORDER A PIZZA....

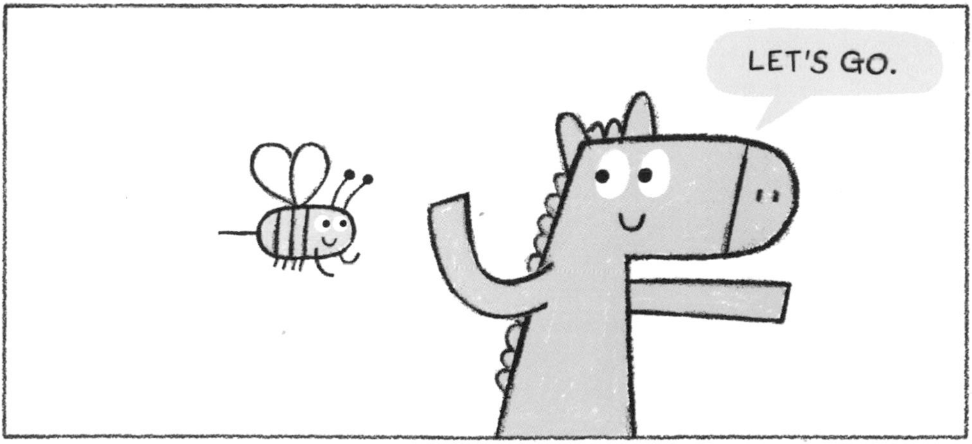
LET'S GO.

MEANWHILE, BACKSTAGE . . .

AHA! HERE IT IS!

MAGIC STUFF

PRESTO! MAGIC DISAPPEARING IDEA

MORE MAGIC

PRESTO! MAGIC DISAPPEARING POWDER

IT WORKS!

NOW I'LL SHOW THOSE PESKY NONBELIEVERS.

POOF!

PRESTO MAGIC DISAPPEARING POWDER

STAGE

I WILL MAKE THEM ALL . . .

. . . DISAPPEAR?

PRESTO MAGIC

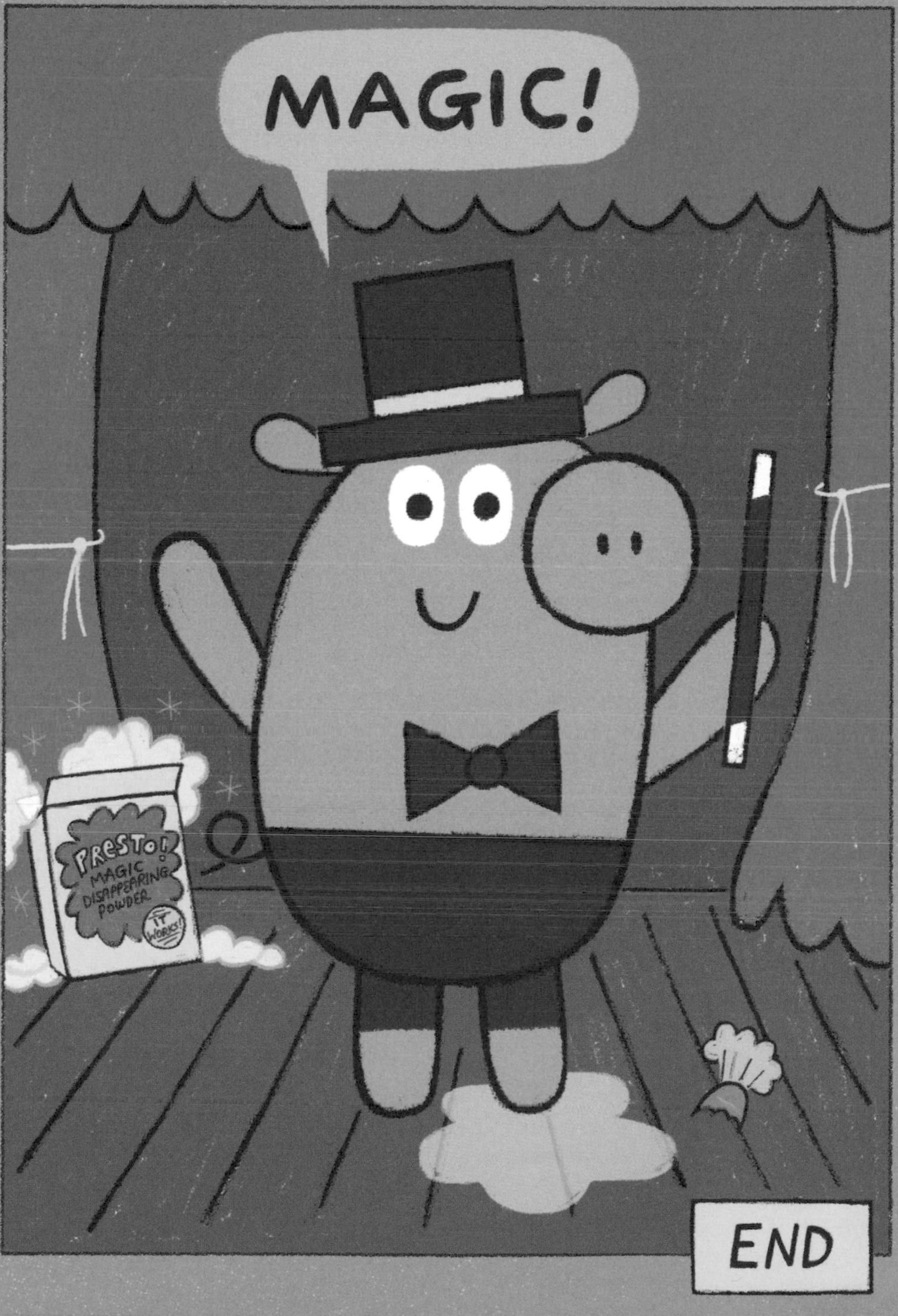
MAGIC!
PRESTO!
MAGIC
DISAPPEARING
POWDER
IT WORKS!
END

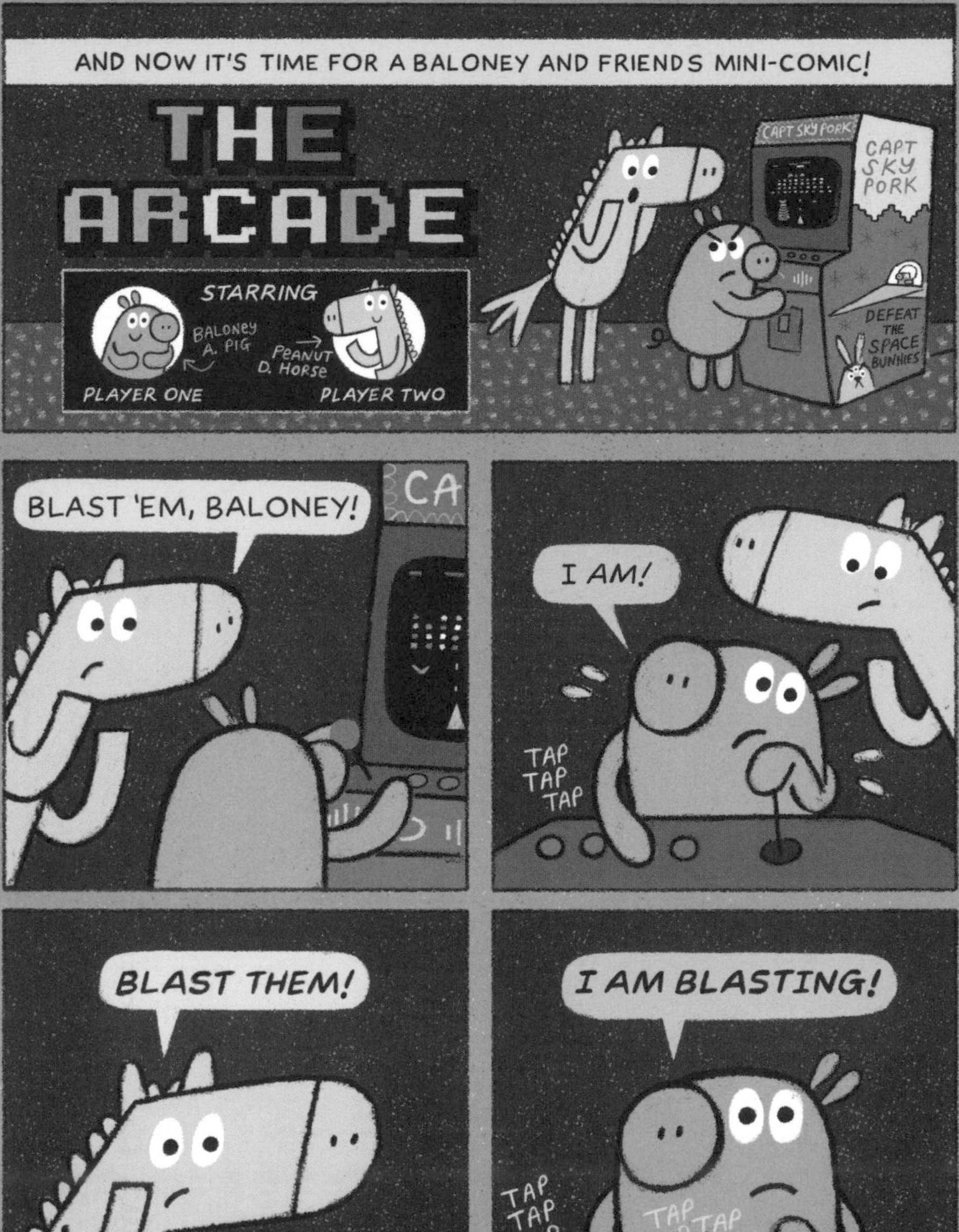
AND NOW IT'S TIME FOR A BALONEY AND FRIENDS MINI-COMIC!
THE ARCADE
STARRING
BALONEY A. PIG
PEANUT D. HORSE
PLAYER ONE
PLAYER TWO
CAPT SKY PORK
CAPT SKY PORK
DEFEAT THE SPACE BUNNIES
BLAST 'EM, BALONEY!
I AM!
TAP TAP TAP
BLAST THEM!
I AM BLASTING!
TAP TAP TAP
TAP TAP TAP

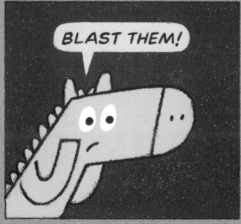

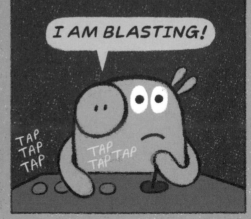

END

35

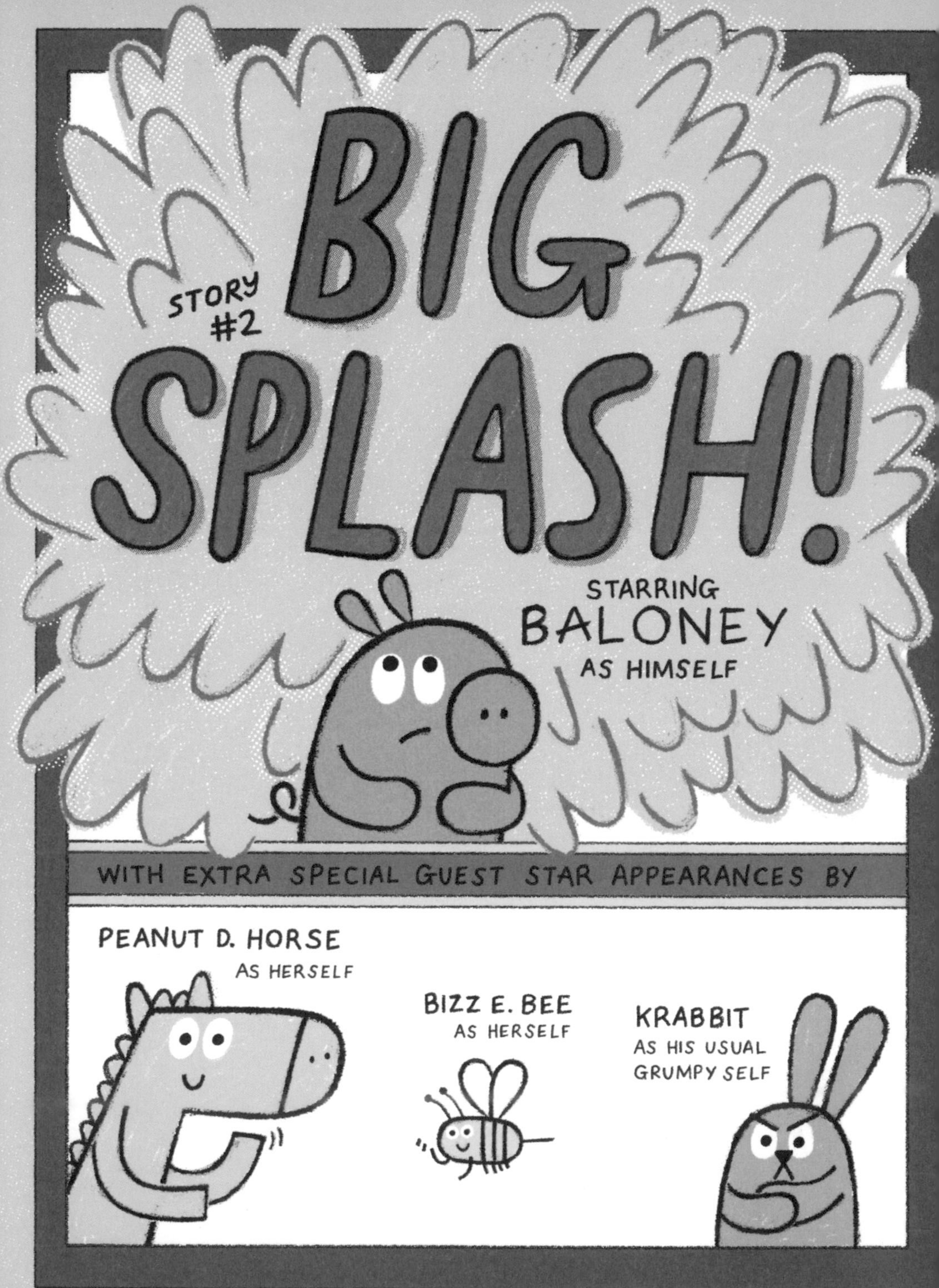
STORY #2
BIG SPLASH!
STARRING
BALONEY
AS HIMSELF
WITH EXTRA SPECIAL GUEST STAR APPEARANCES BY
PEANUT D. HORSE
AS HERSELF
BIZZ E. BEE
AS HERSELF
KRABBIT
AS HIS USUAL
GRUMPY SELF

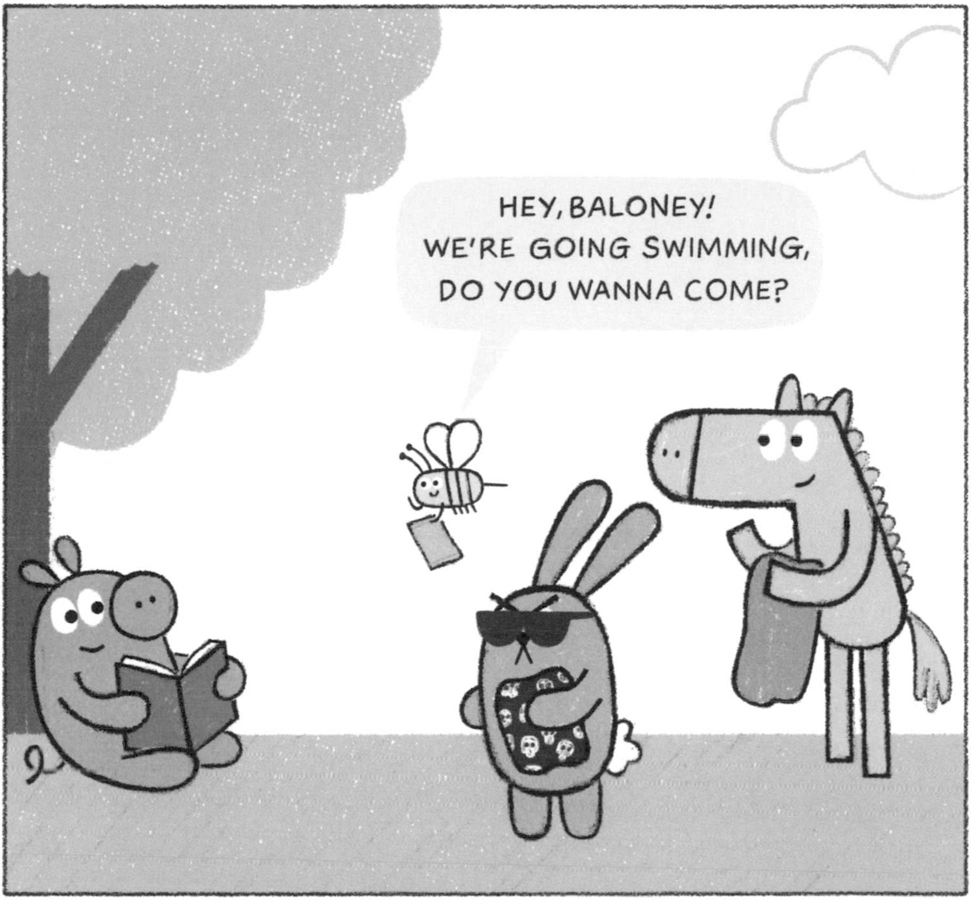
HEY, BALONEY!
WE'RE GOING SWIMMING,
DO YOU WANNA COME?

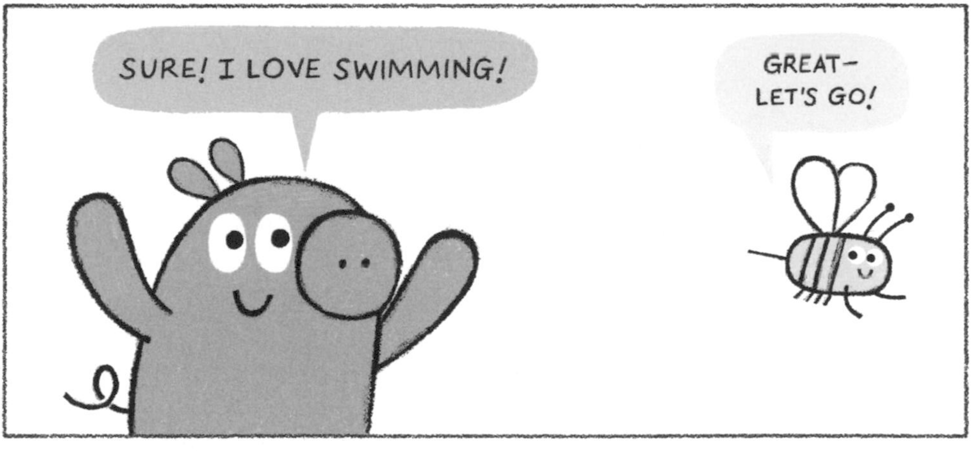
SURE! I LOVE SWIMMING!
GREAT—
LET'S GO!

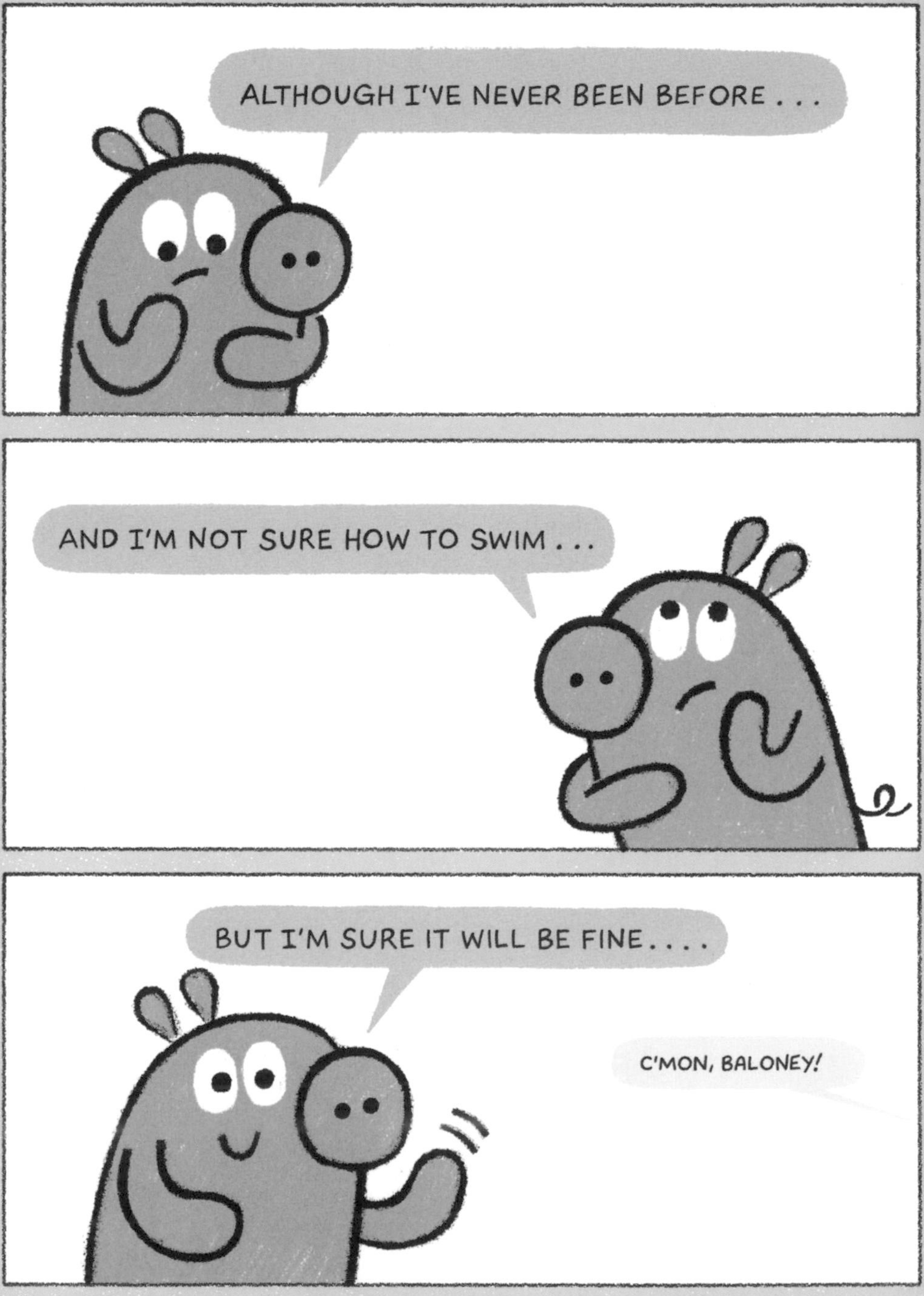
ALTHOUGH I'VE NEVER BEEN BEFORE . . .
AND I'M NOT SURE HOW TO SWIM . . .
BUT I'M SURE IT WILL BE FINE . . . .
C'MON, BALONEY!

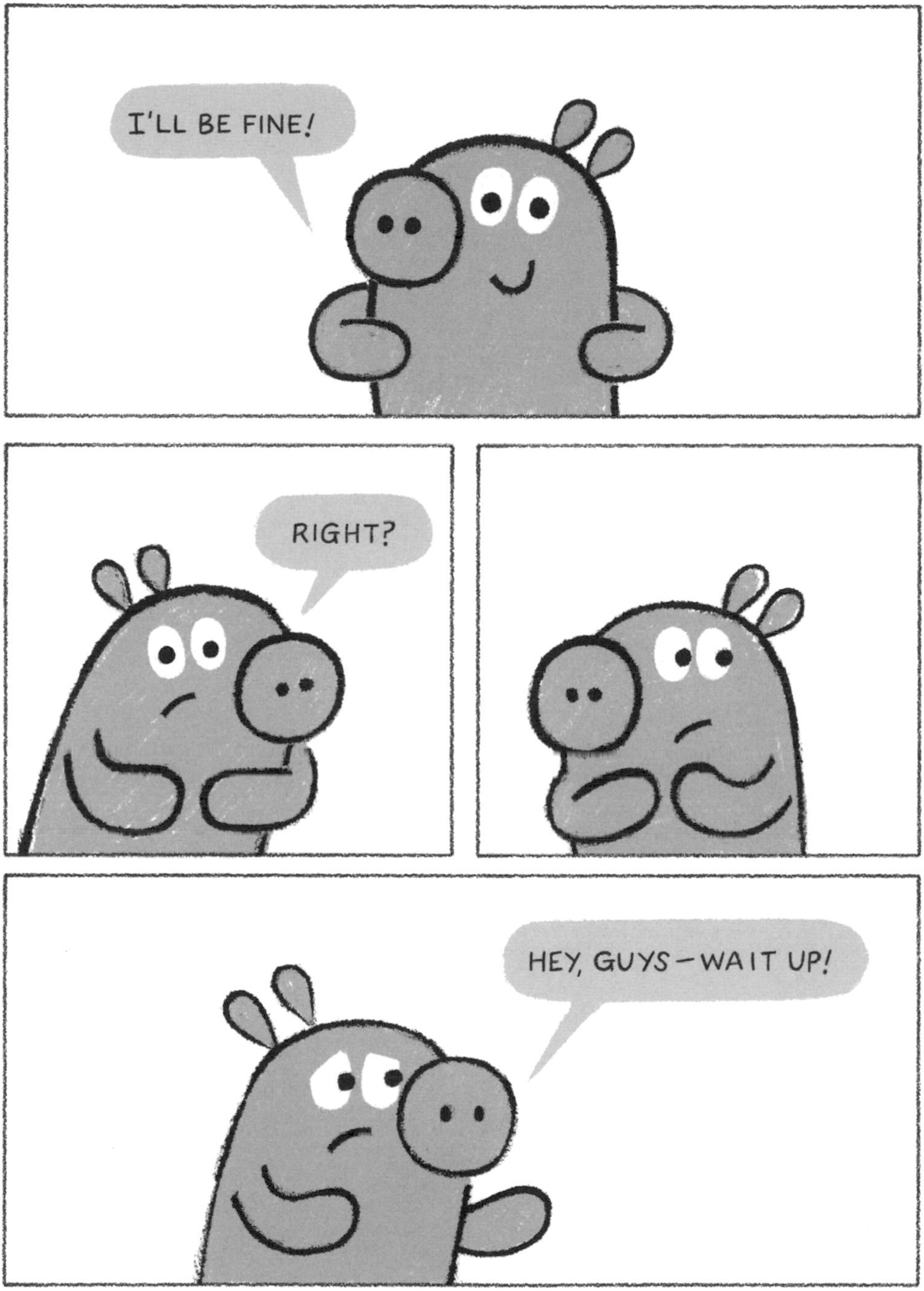
I'LL BE FINE!
RIGHT?
HEY, GUYS—WAIT UP!

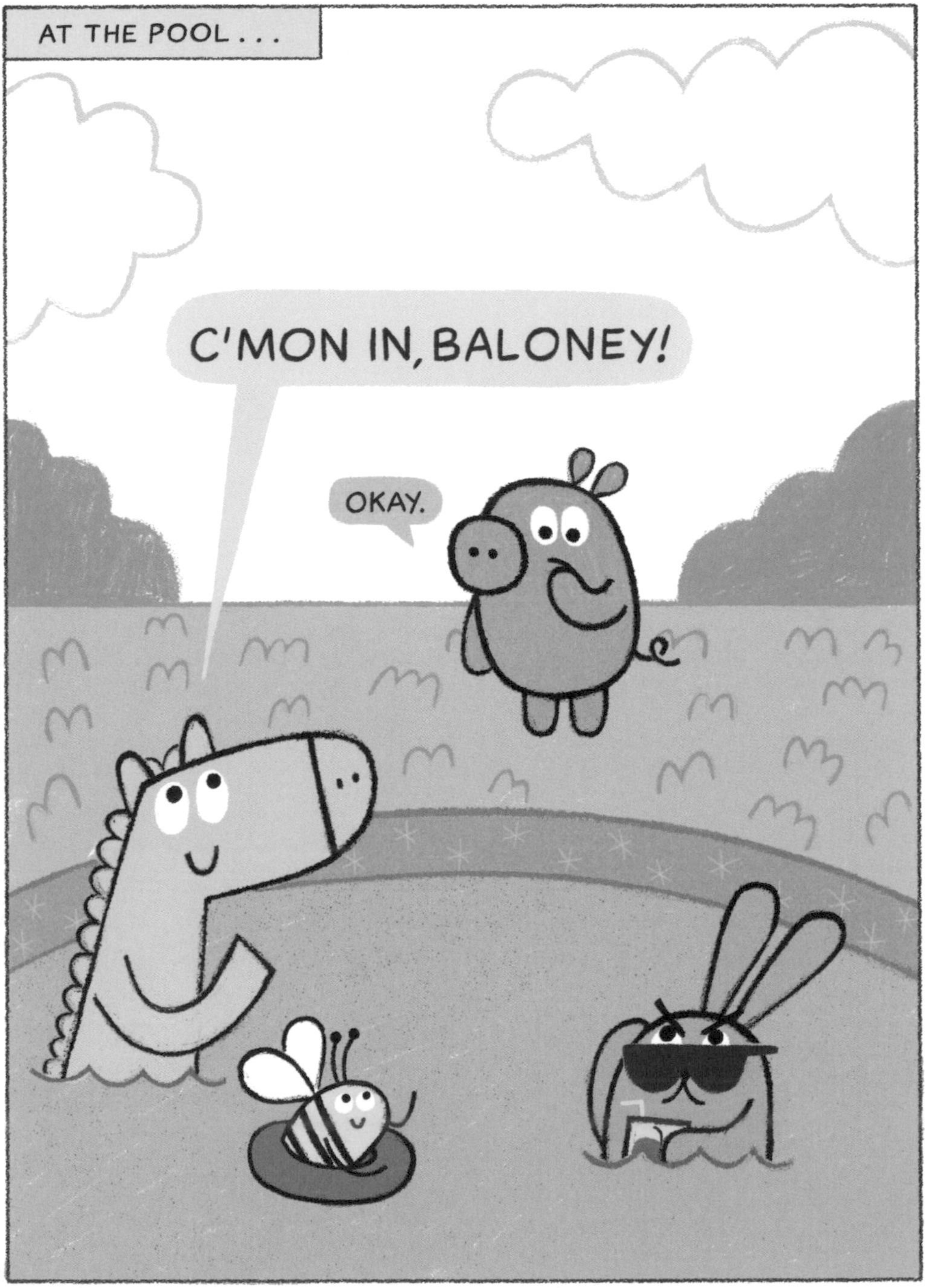
AT THE POOL . . .
C'MON IN, BALONEY!
OKAY.

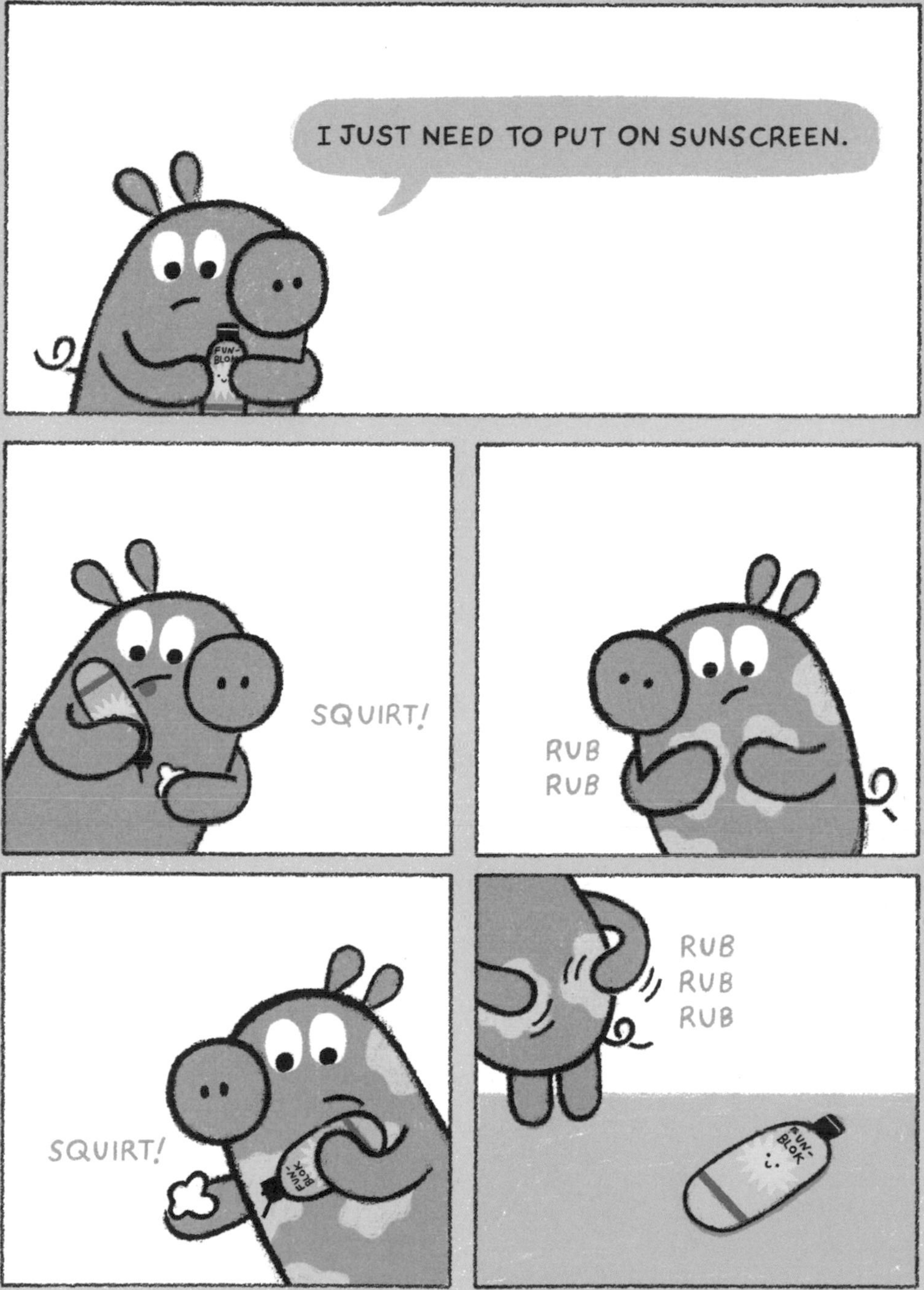
I JUST NEED TO PUT ON SUNSCREEN.
FUN-BLOK
SQUIRT!
RUB
RUB
SQUIRT!
FUN-BLOK
RUB
RUB
RUB
FUN-BLOK

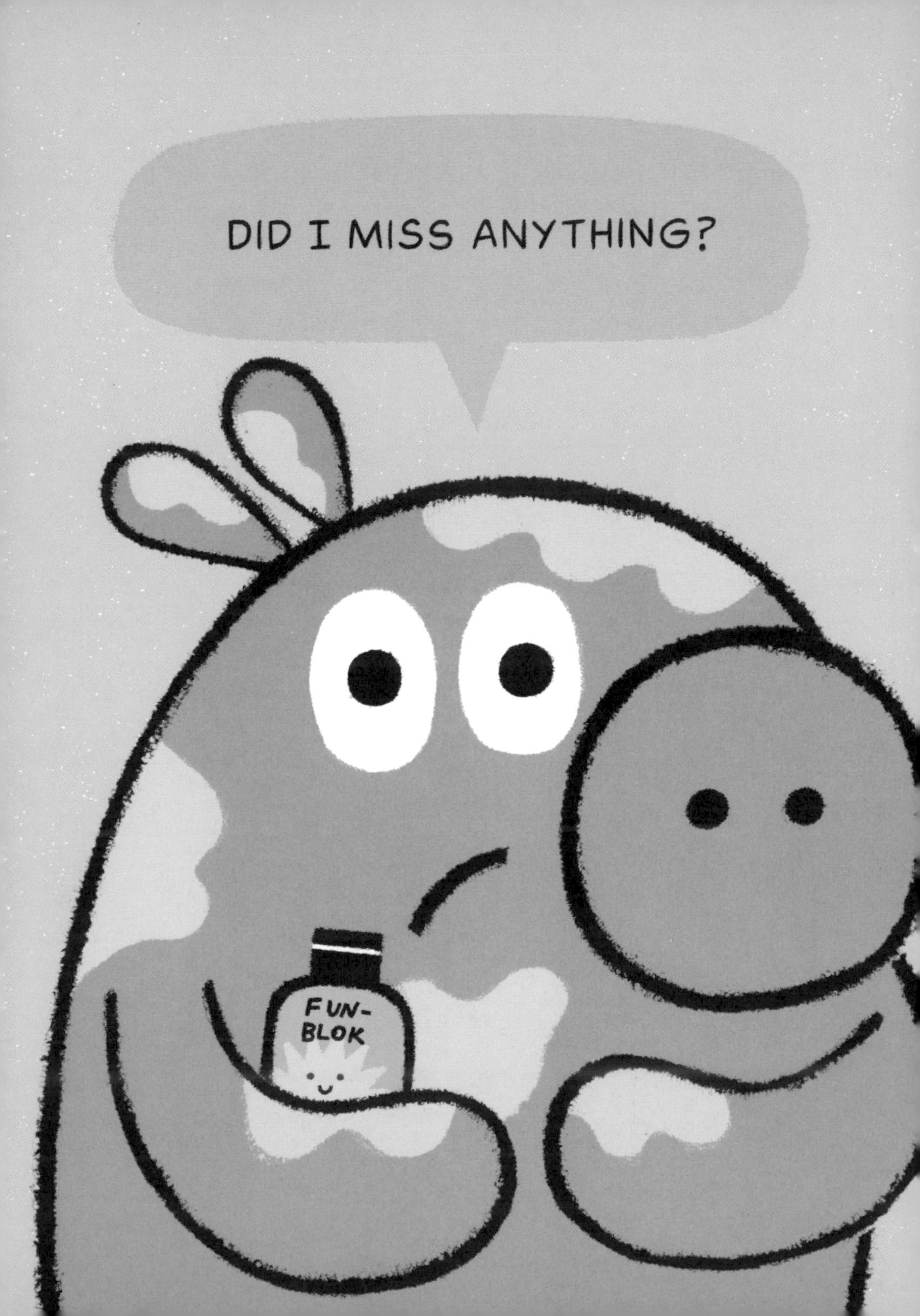
DID I MISS ANYTHING?
FUN-
BLOK

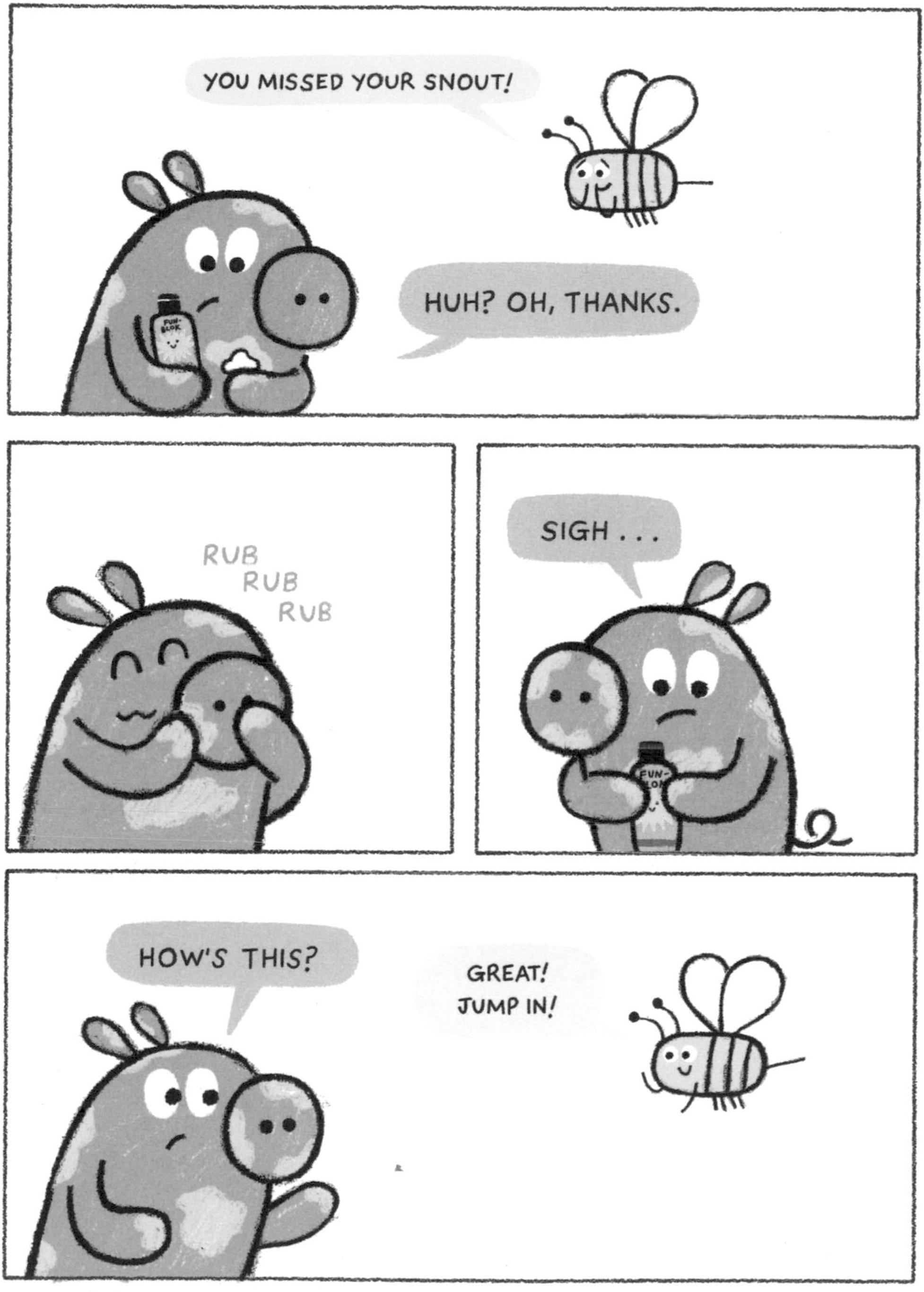
YOU MISSED YOUR SNOUT!
HUH? OH, THANKS.
RUB
RUB
RUB
SIGH . . .
HOW'S THIS?
GREAT!
JUMP IN!

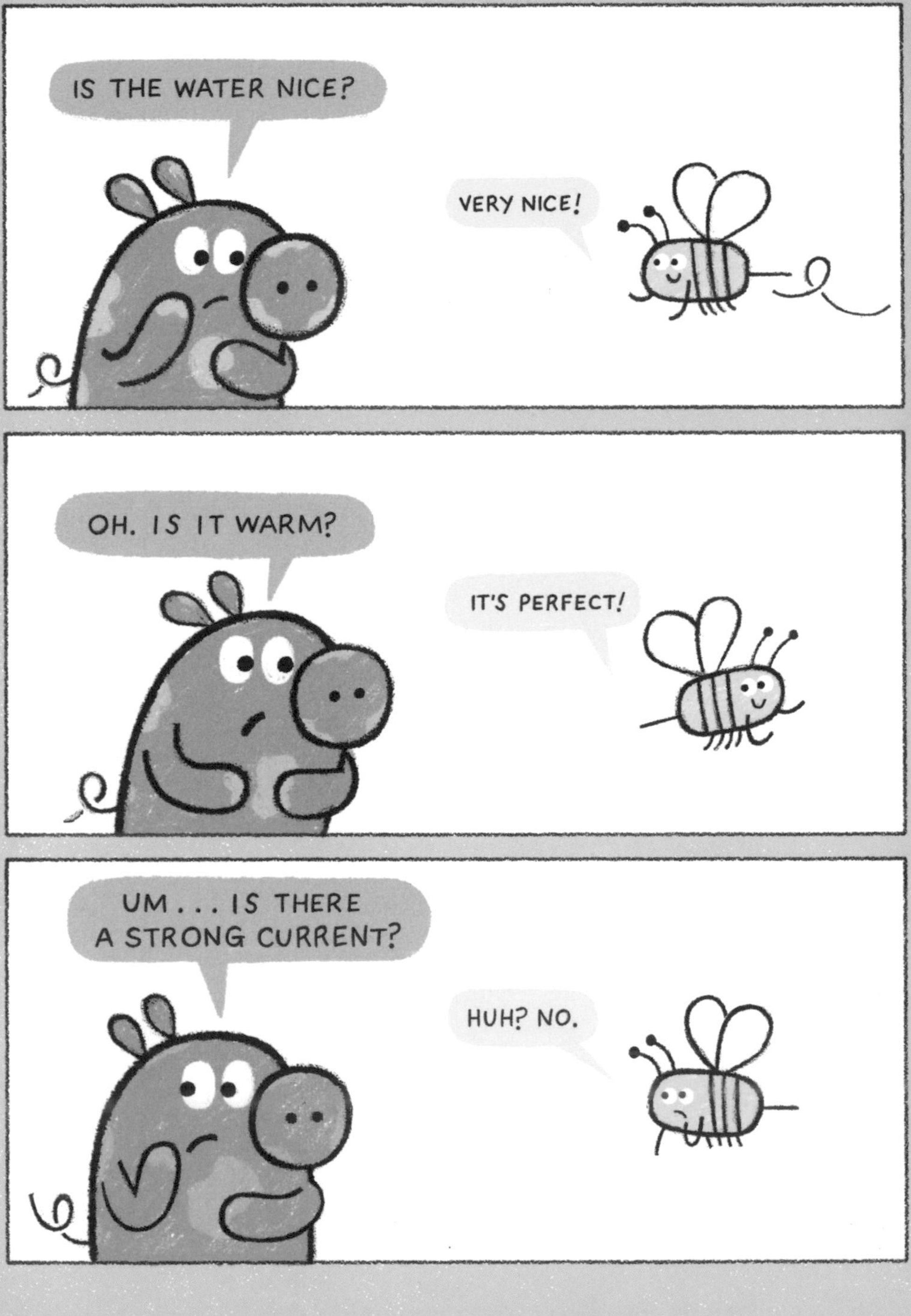
IS THE WATER NICE?
VERY NICE!
OH. IS IT WARM?
IT'S PERFECT!
UM . . . IS THERE A STRONG CURRENT?
HUH? NO.

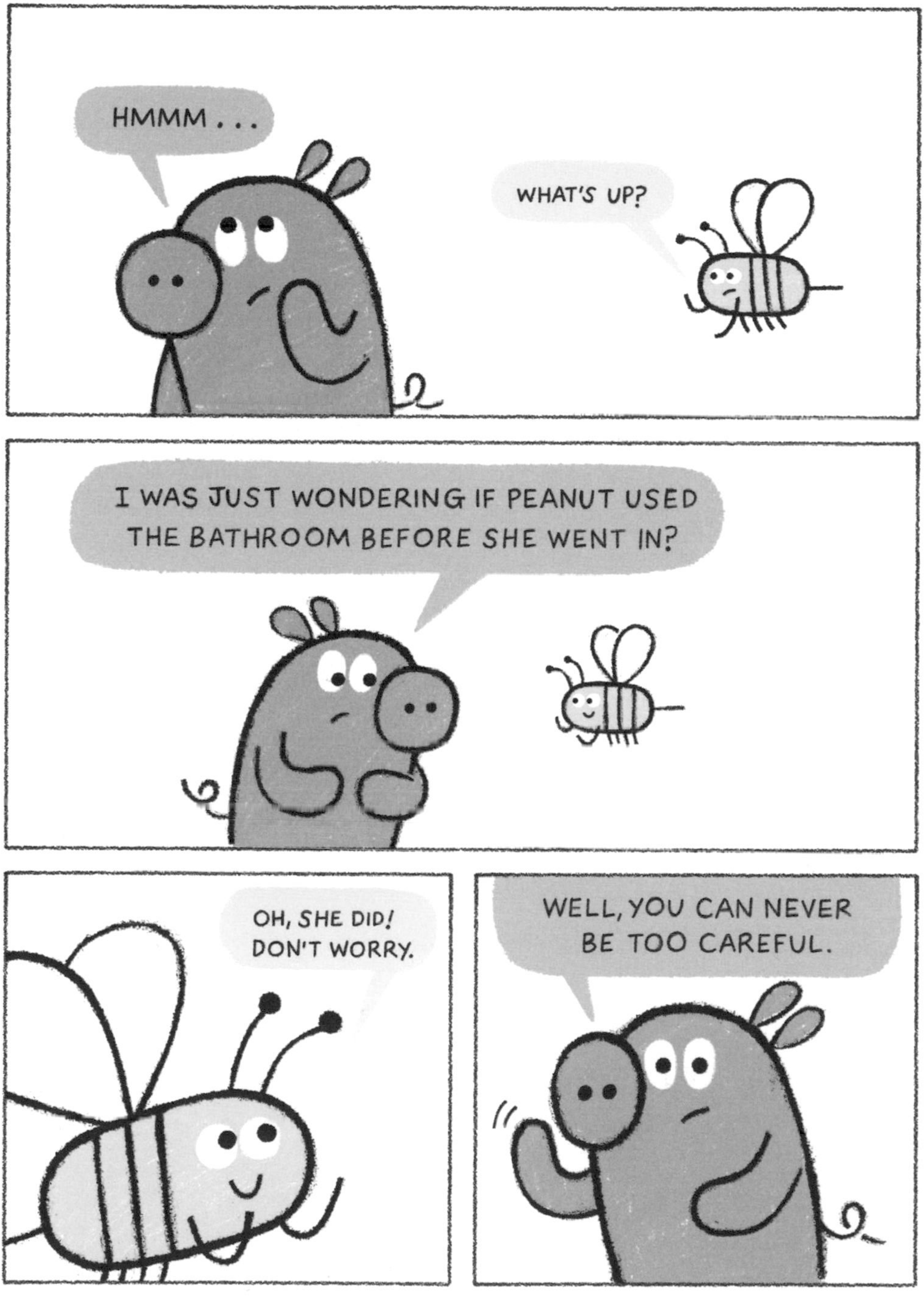
HMMM . . .
WHAT'S UP?
I WAS JUST WONDERING IF PEANUT USED THE BATHROOM BEFORE SHE WENT IN?
OH, SHE DID! DON'T WORRY.
WELL, YOU CAN NEVER BE TOO CAREFUL.

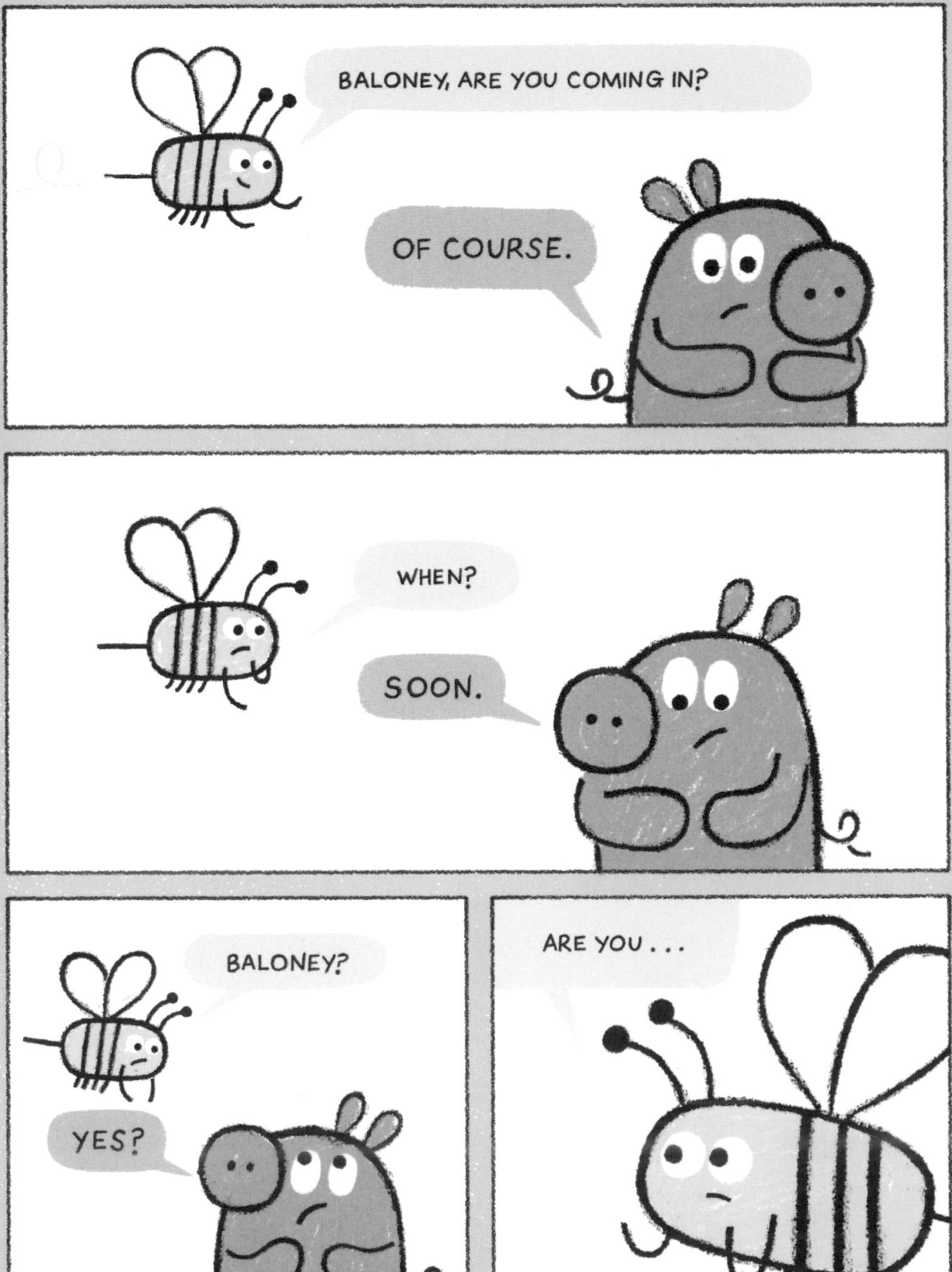
BALONEY, ARE YOU COMING IN?
OF COURSE.
WHEN?
SOON.
BALONEY?
YES?
ARE YOU . . .

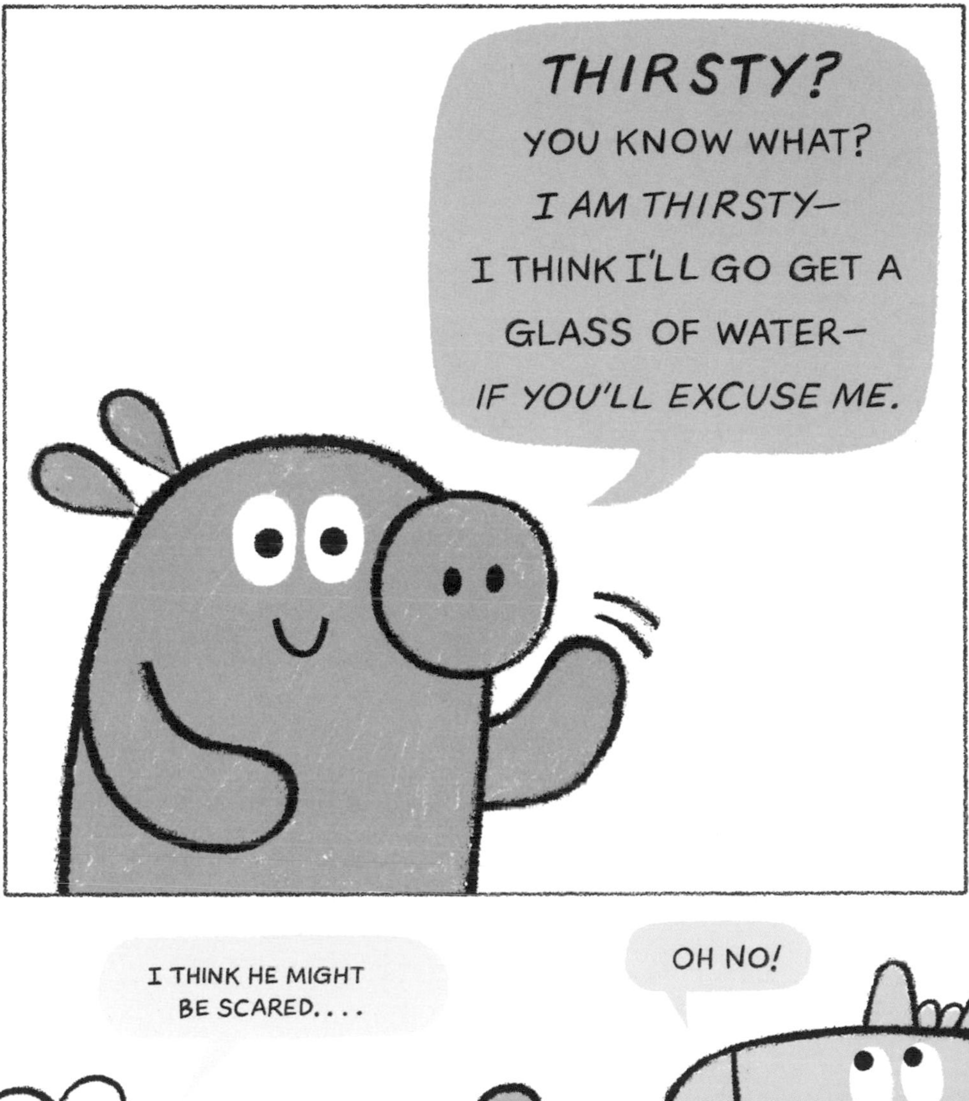
THIRSTY?
YOU KNOW WHAT?
I AM THIRSTY—
I THINK I'LL GO GET A
GLASS OF WATER—
IF YOU'LL EXCUSE ME.

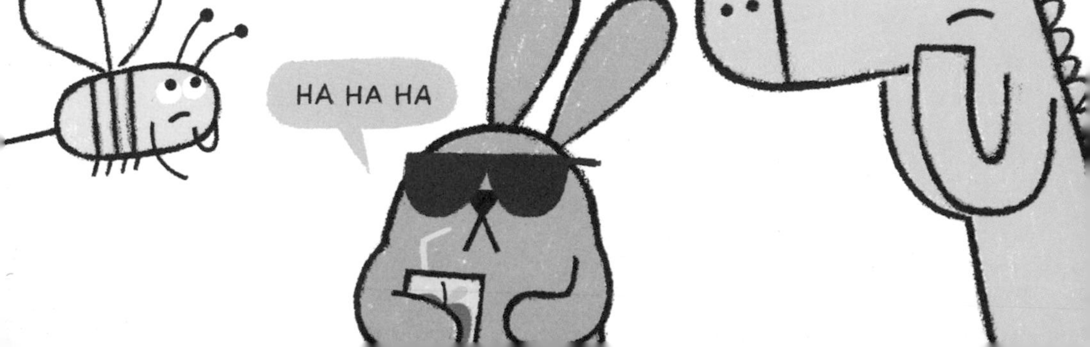
I THINK HE MIGHT BE SCARED. . . .
OH NO!
HA HA HA

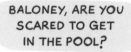

BALONEY, ARE YOU SCARED TO GET IN THE POOL?

ME? NO WAY! I'M NOT SCARED OF THE POOL....

I AM, HOWEVER, A LITTLE CONCERNED ABOUT THOSE STORM CLOUDS.

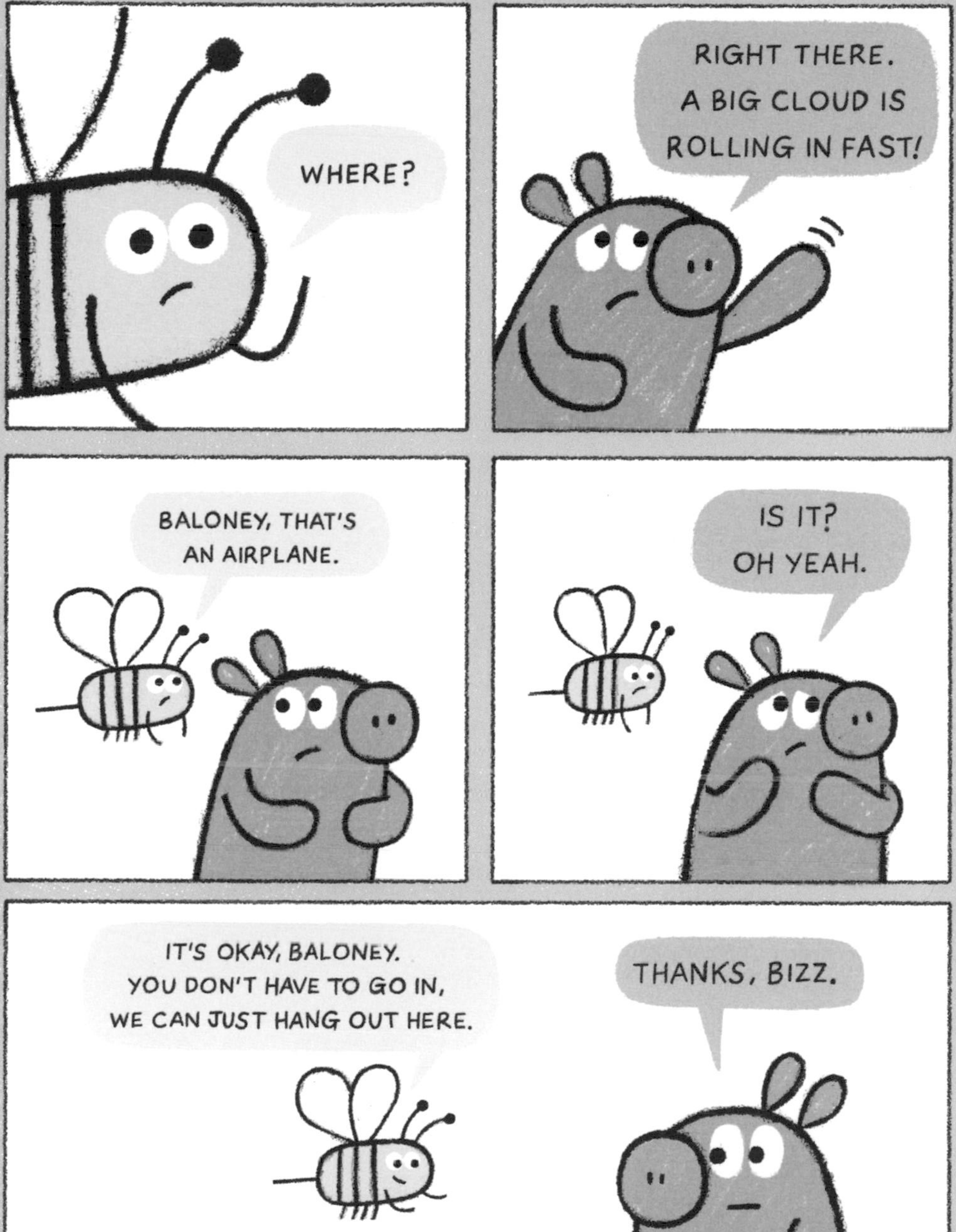
WHERE?
RIGHT THERE. A BIG CLOUD IS ROLLING IN FAST!
BALONEY, THAT'S AN AIRPLANE.
IS IT? OH YEAH.
IT'S OKAY, BALONEY. YOU DON'T HAVE TO GO IN, WE CAN JUST HANG OUT HERE.
THANKS, BIZZ.

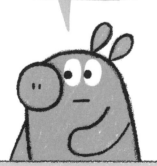

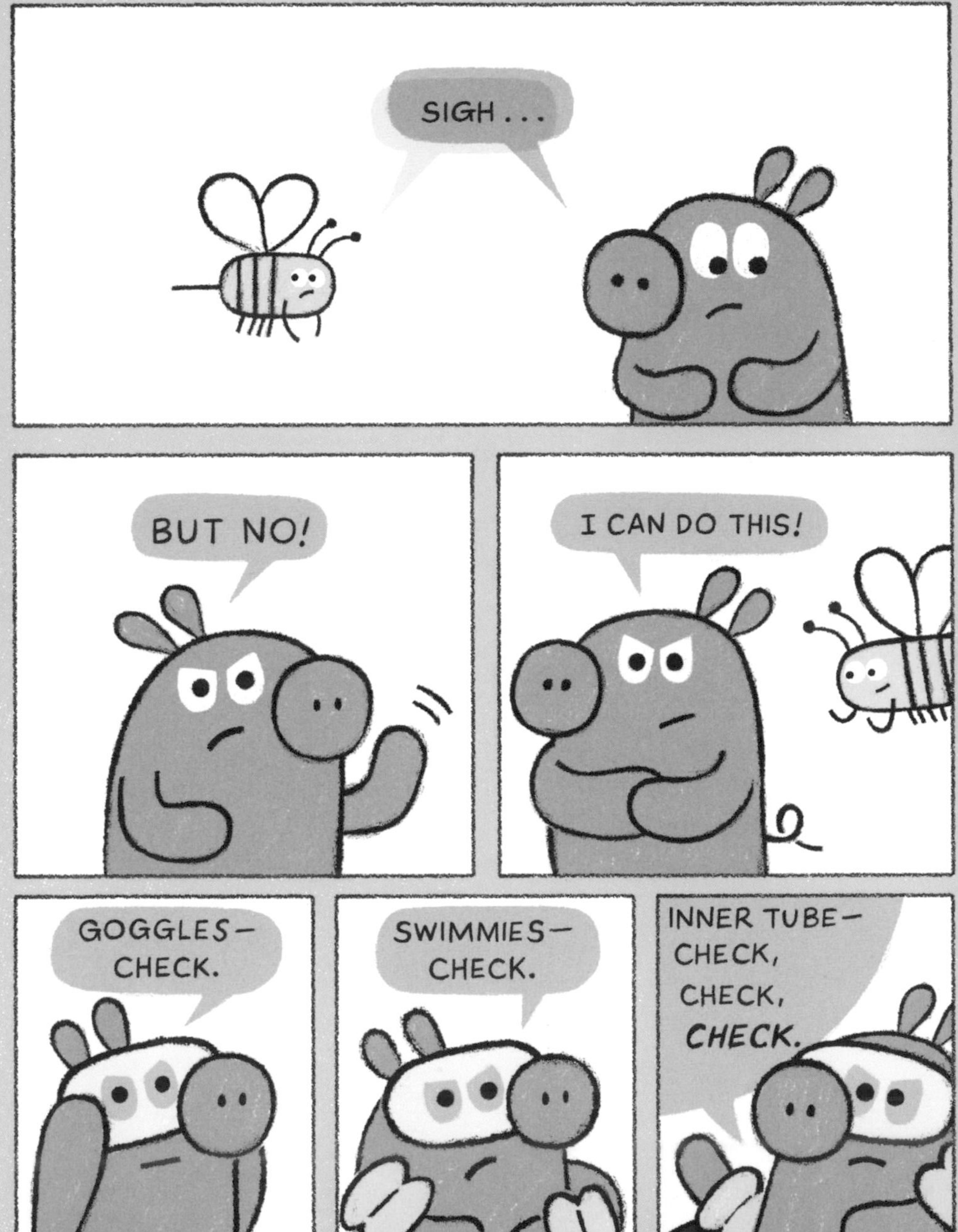
SIGH . . .
BUT NO!
I CAN DO THIS!
GOGGLES—
CHECK.
SWIMMIES—
CHECK.
INNER TUBE—
CHECK,
CHECK,
CHECK.

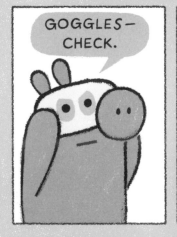

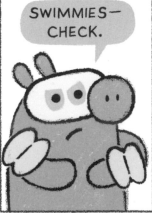

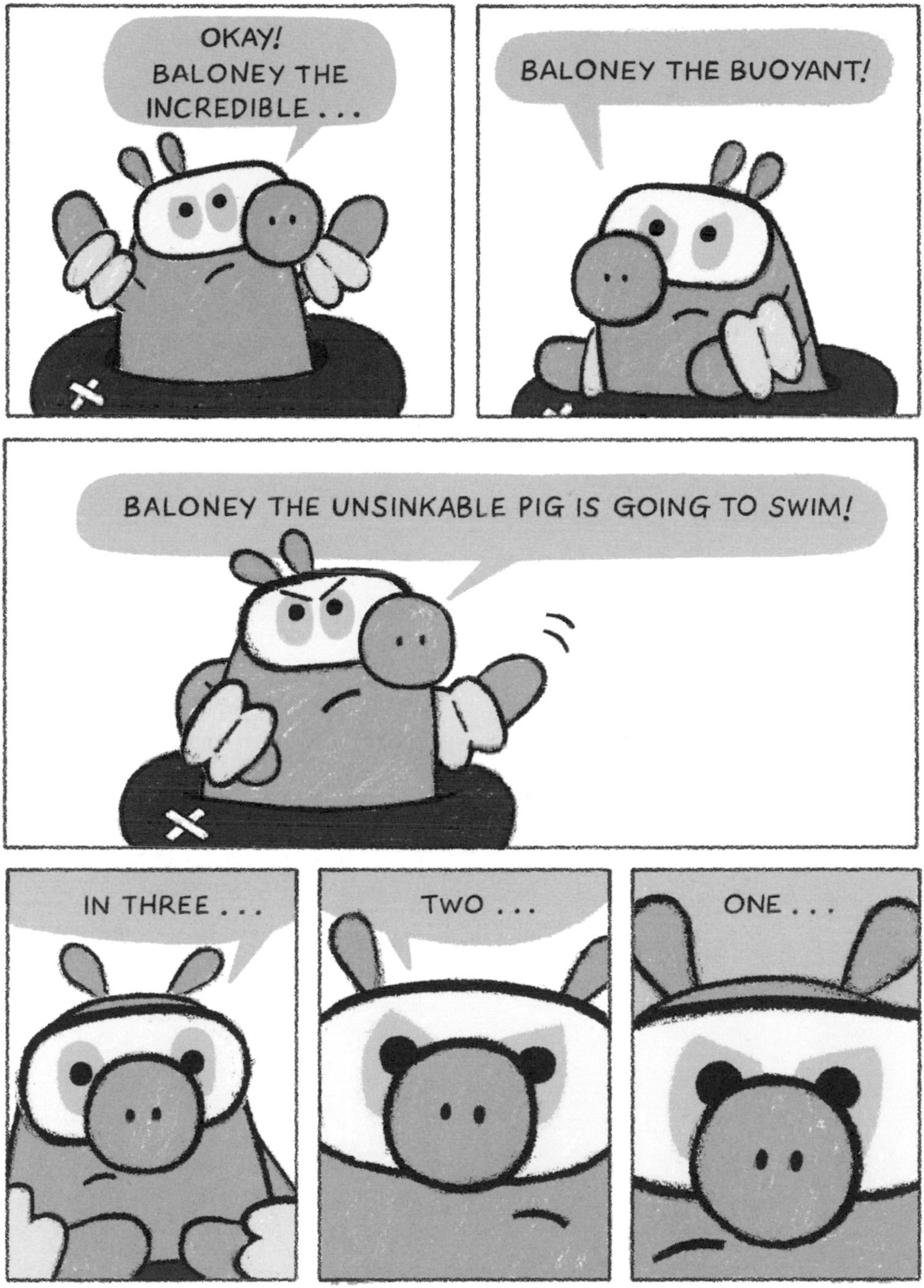
OKAY!
BALONEY THE INCREDIBLE . . .
BALONEY THE BUOYANT!
BALONEY THE UNSINKABLE PIG IS GOING TO SWIM!
IN THREE . . .
TWO . . .
ONE . . .

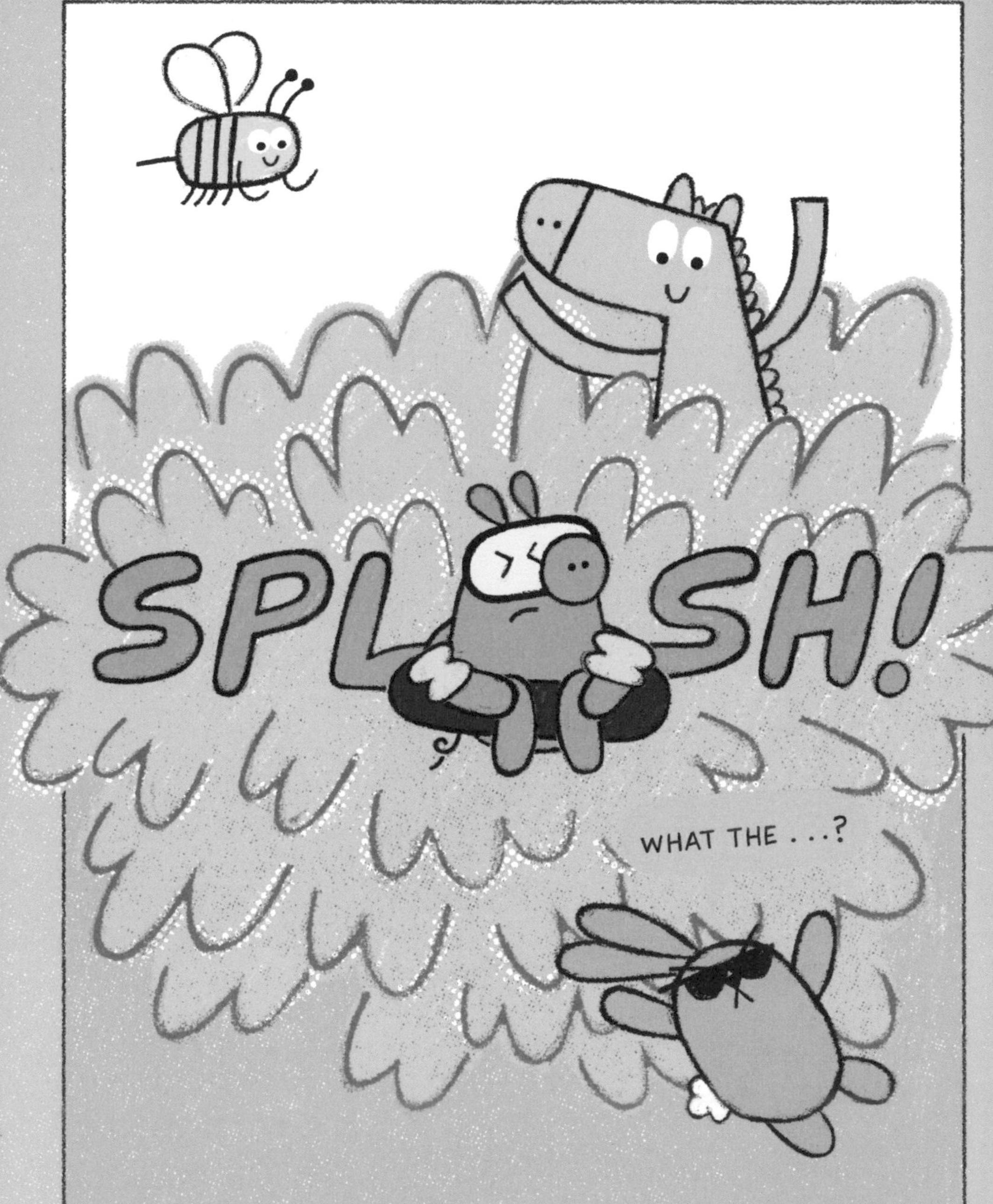
SPL SH!
WHAT THE . . .?

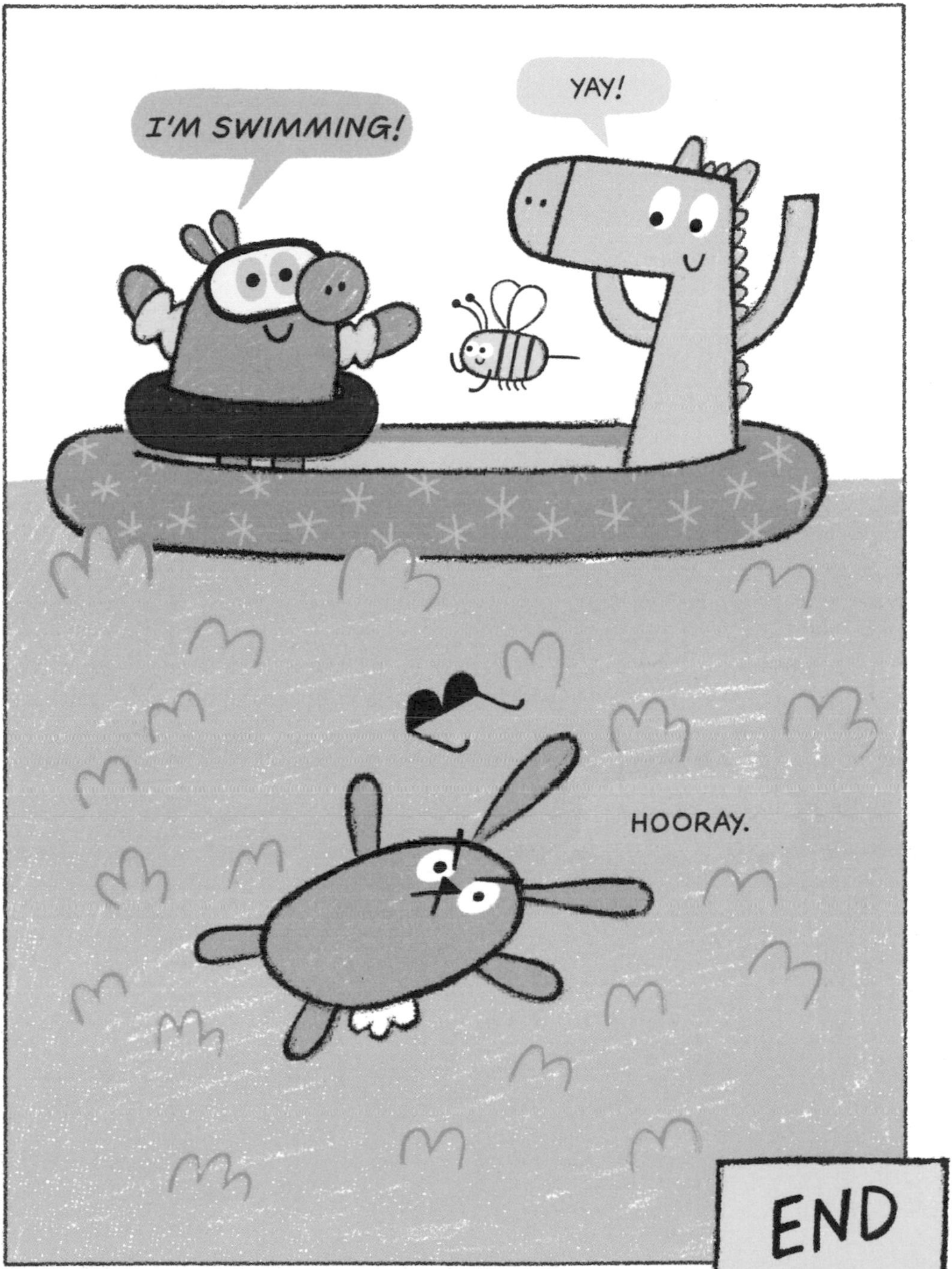
I'M SWIMMING!
YAY!
HOORAY.
END

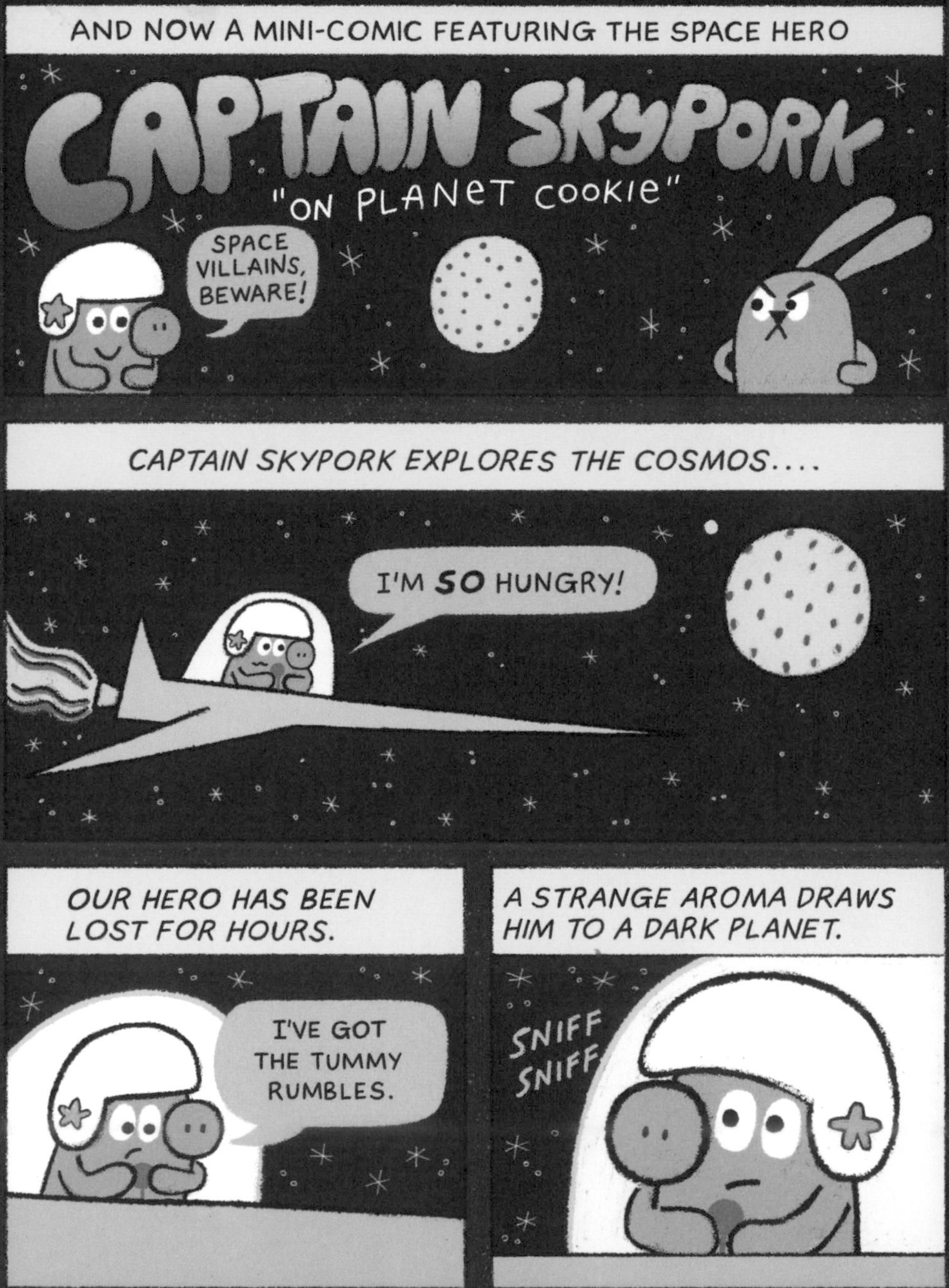
AND NOW A MINI-COMIC FEATURING THE SPACE HERO
CAPTAIN SKYPORK
"ON PLANET COOKIE"
SPACE VILLAINS, BEWARE!
CAPTAIN SKYPORK EXPLORES THE COSMOS....
I'M SO HUNGRY!
OUR HERO HAS BEEN LOST FOR HOURS.
I'VE GOT THE TUMMY RUMBLES.
A STRANGE AROMA DRAWS HIM TO A DARK PLANET.
SNIFF SNIFF

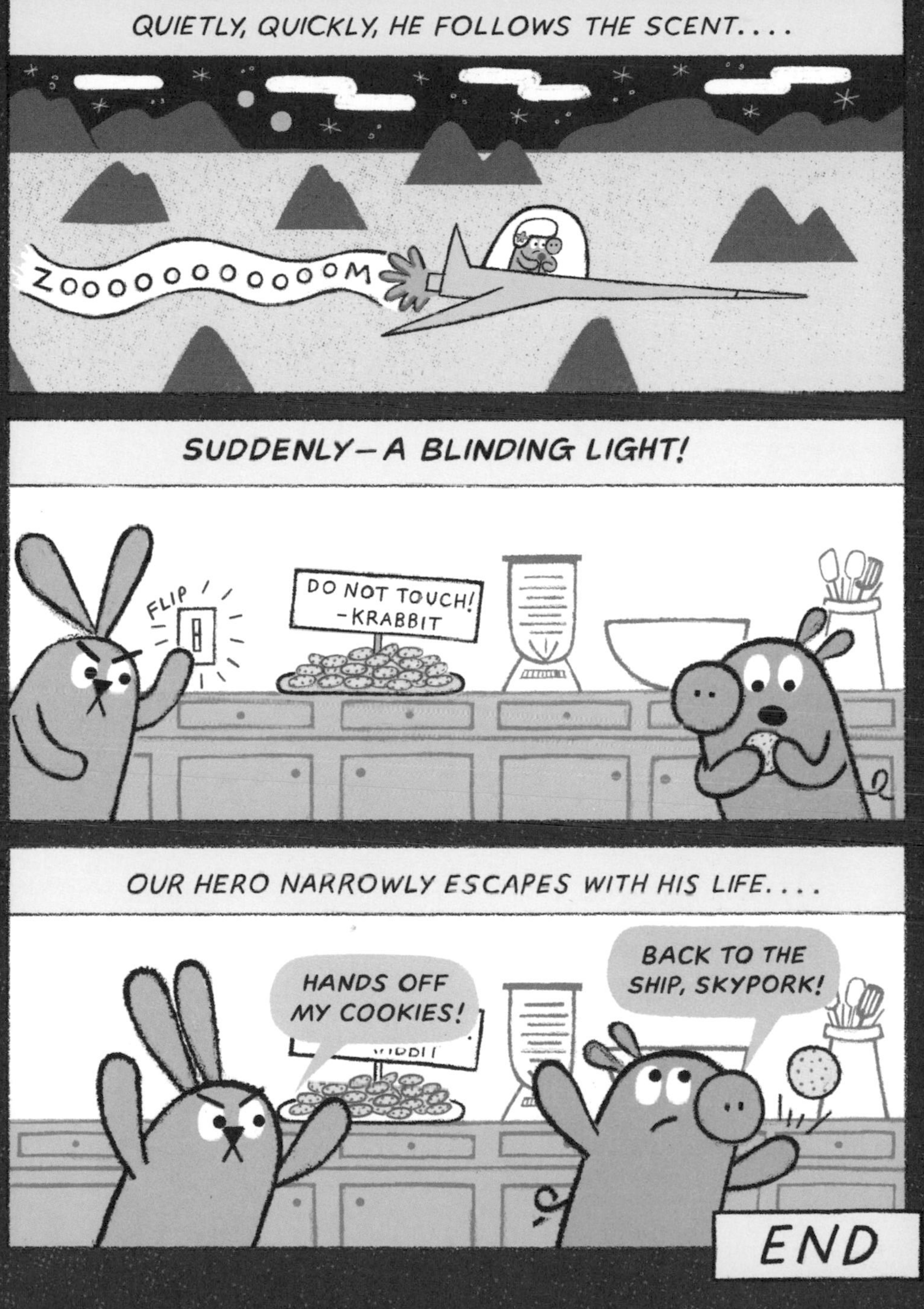

QUIETLY, QUICKLY, HE FOLLOWS THE SCENT....
ZOOOOOOOOOOOOOM
SUDDENLY—A BLINDING LIGHT!
FLIP
DO NOT TOUCH! -KRABBIT
OUR HERO NARROWLY ESCAPES WITH HIS LIFE....
HANDS OFF MY COOKIES!
BACK TO THE SHIP, SKYPORK!
END

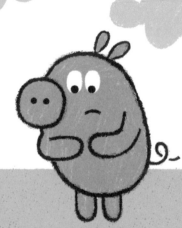

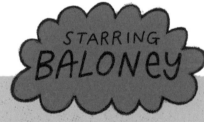

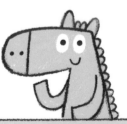

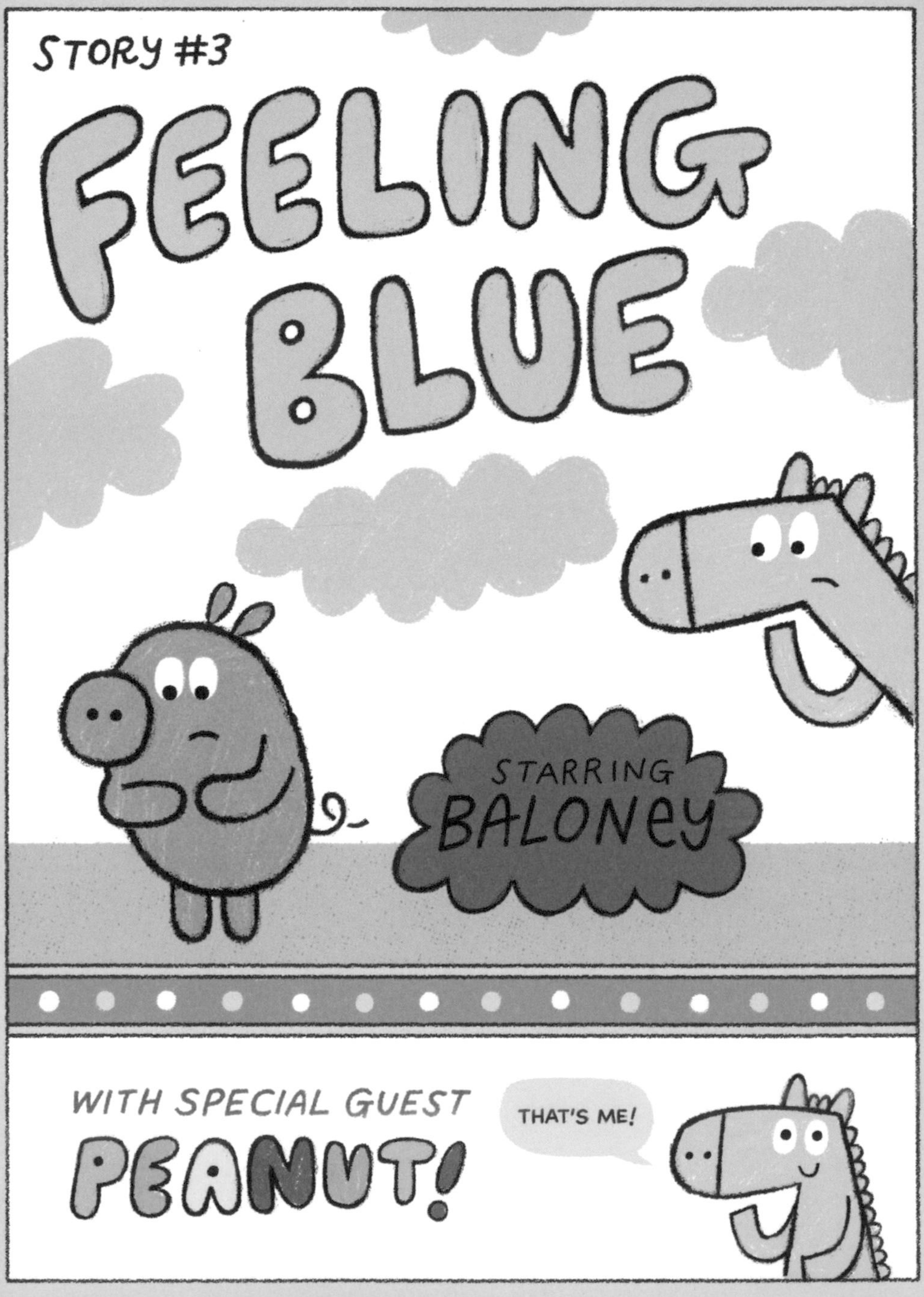
STORY #3
FEELING BLUE
STARRING BALONEY
WITH SPECIAL GUEST
PEANUT!
THAT'S ME!

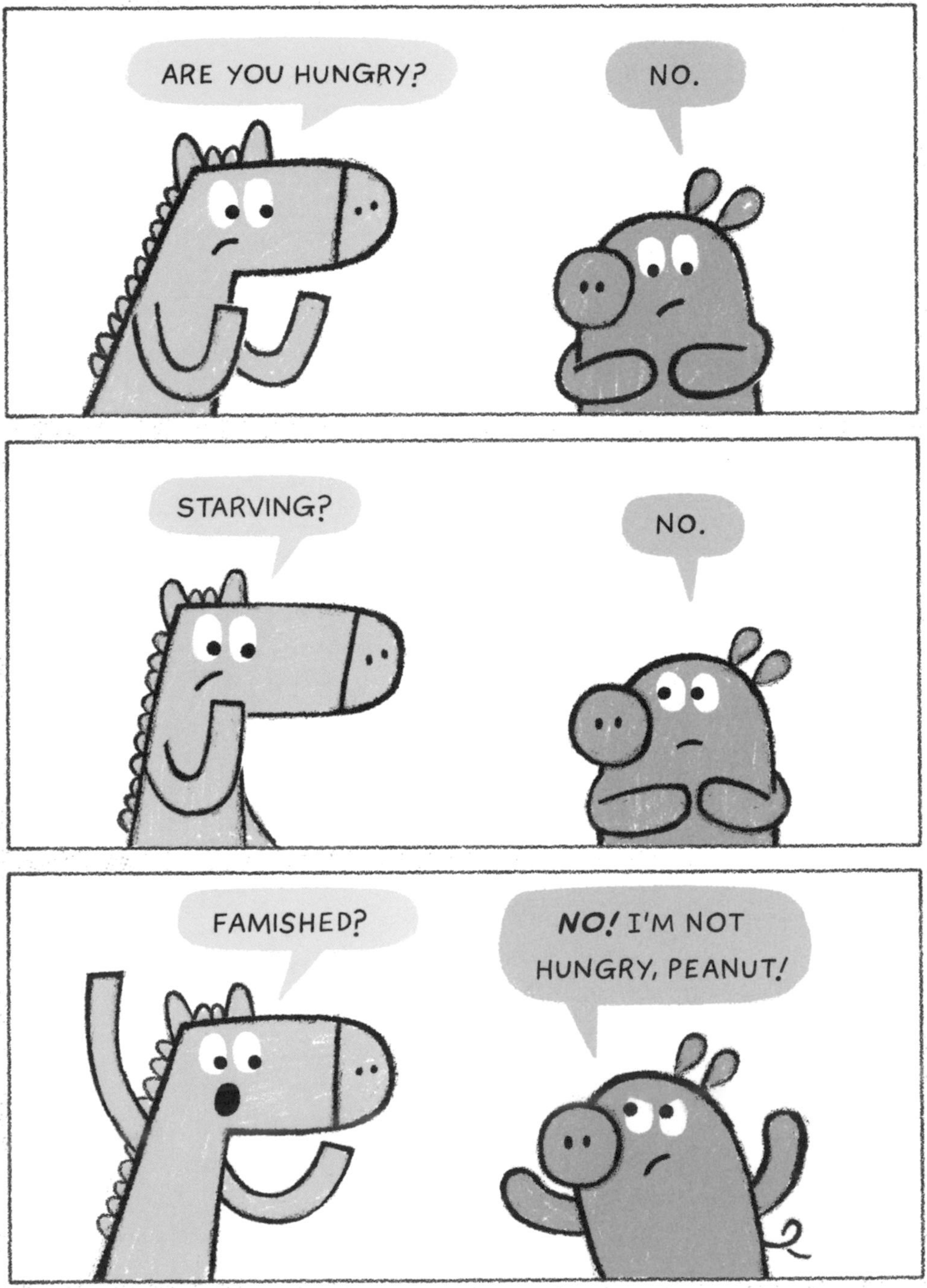
ARE YOU HUNGRY?
NO.
STARVING?
NO.
FAMISHED?
NO! I'M NOT HUNGRY, PEANUT!

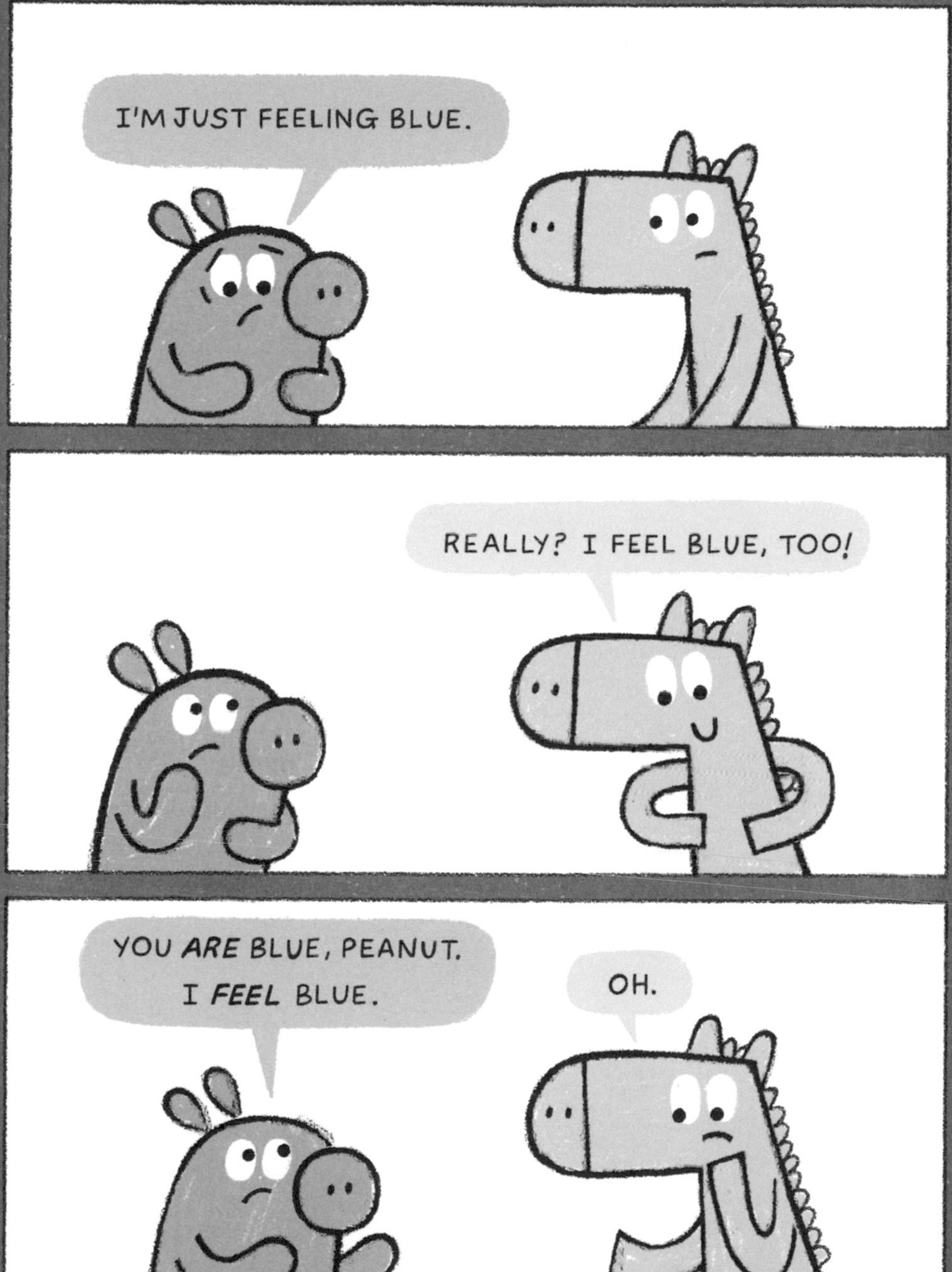
I'M JUST FEELING BLUE.
REALLY? I FEEL BLUE, TOO!
YOU *ARE* BLUE, PEANUT. I *FEEL* BLUE.
OH.

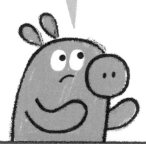

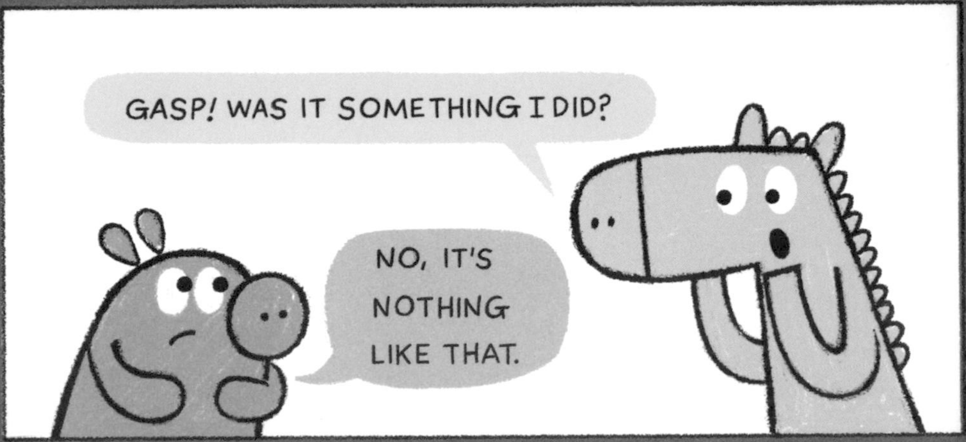
GASP! WAS IT SOMETHING I DID?
NO, IT'S NOTHING LIKE THAT.

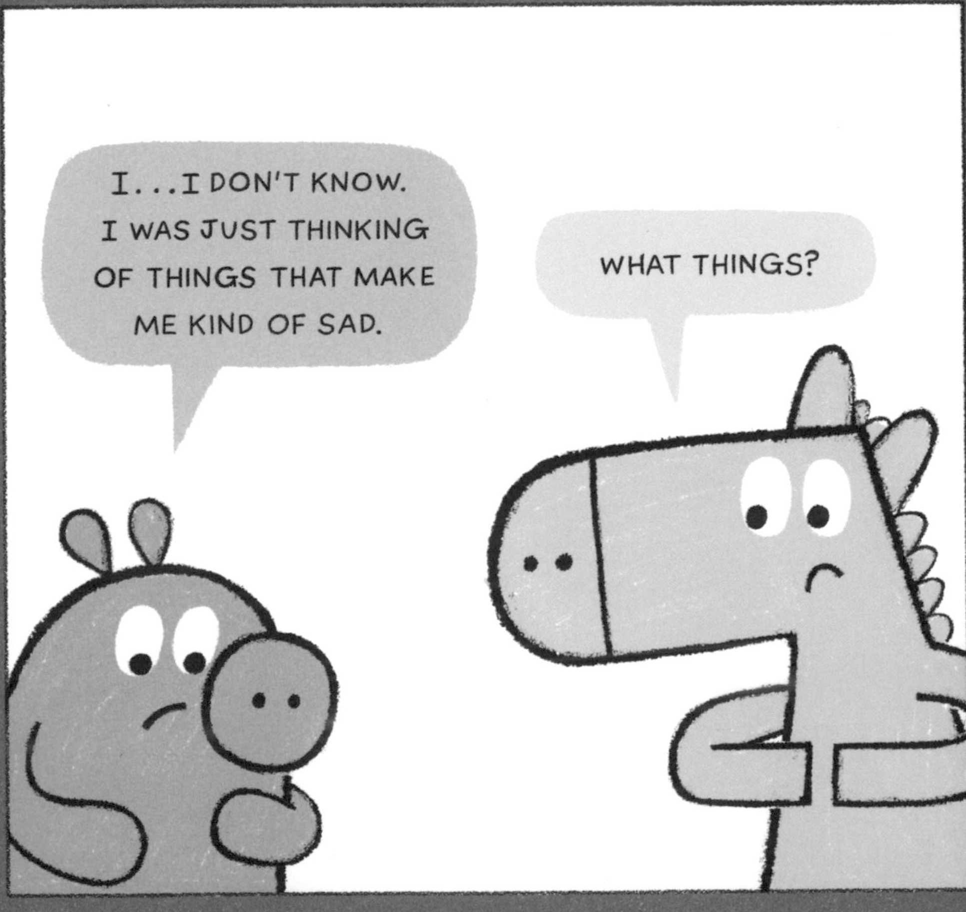
I...I DON'T KNOW. I WAS JUST THINKING OF THINGS THAT MAKE ME KIND OF SAD.
WHAT THINGS?

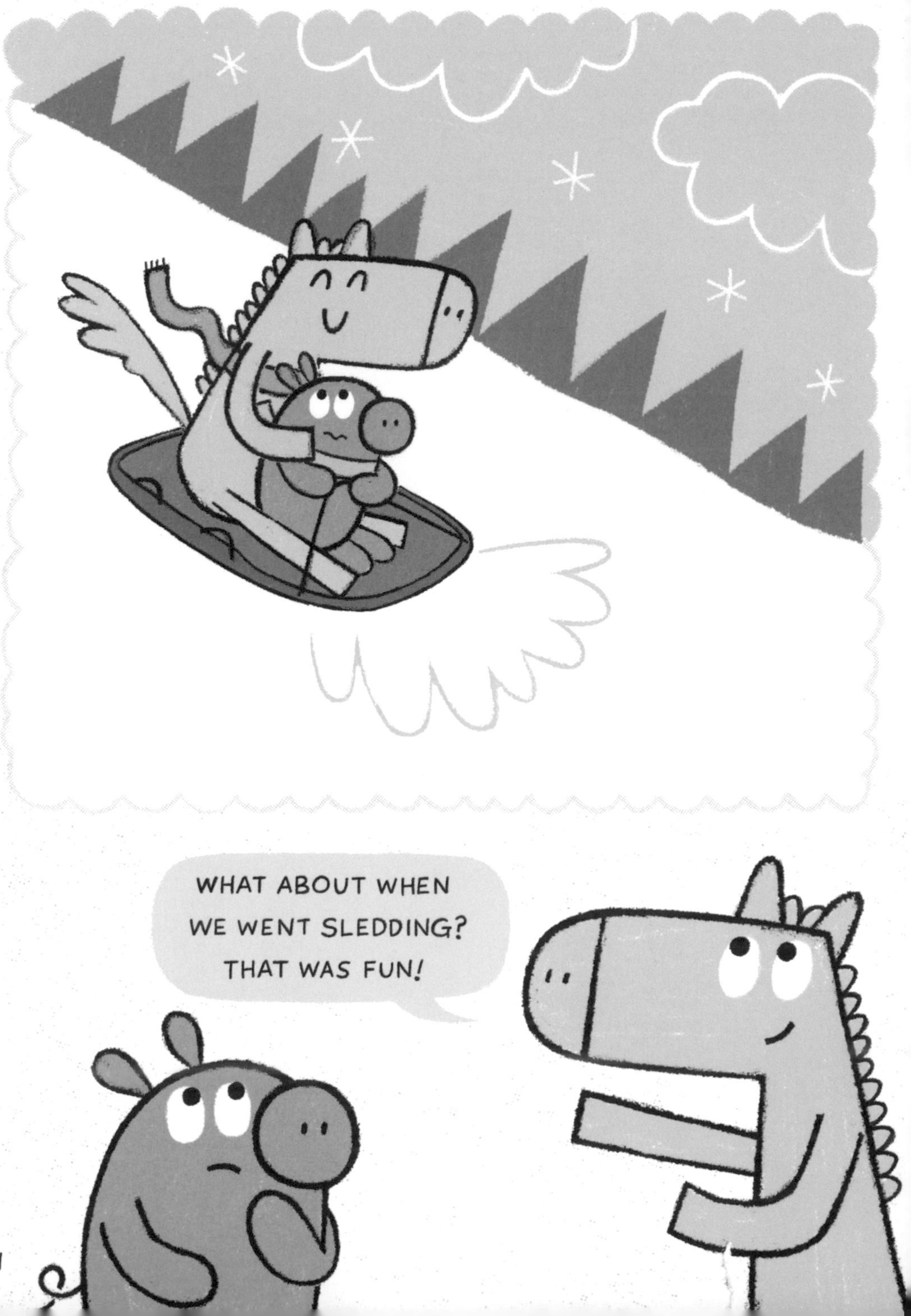
WHAT ABOUT WHEN WE WENT SLEDDING? THAT WAS FUN!

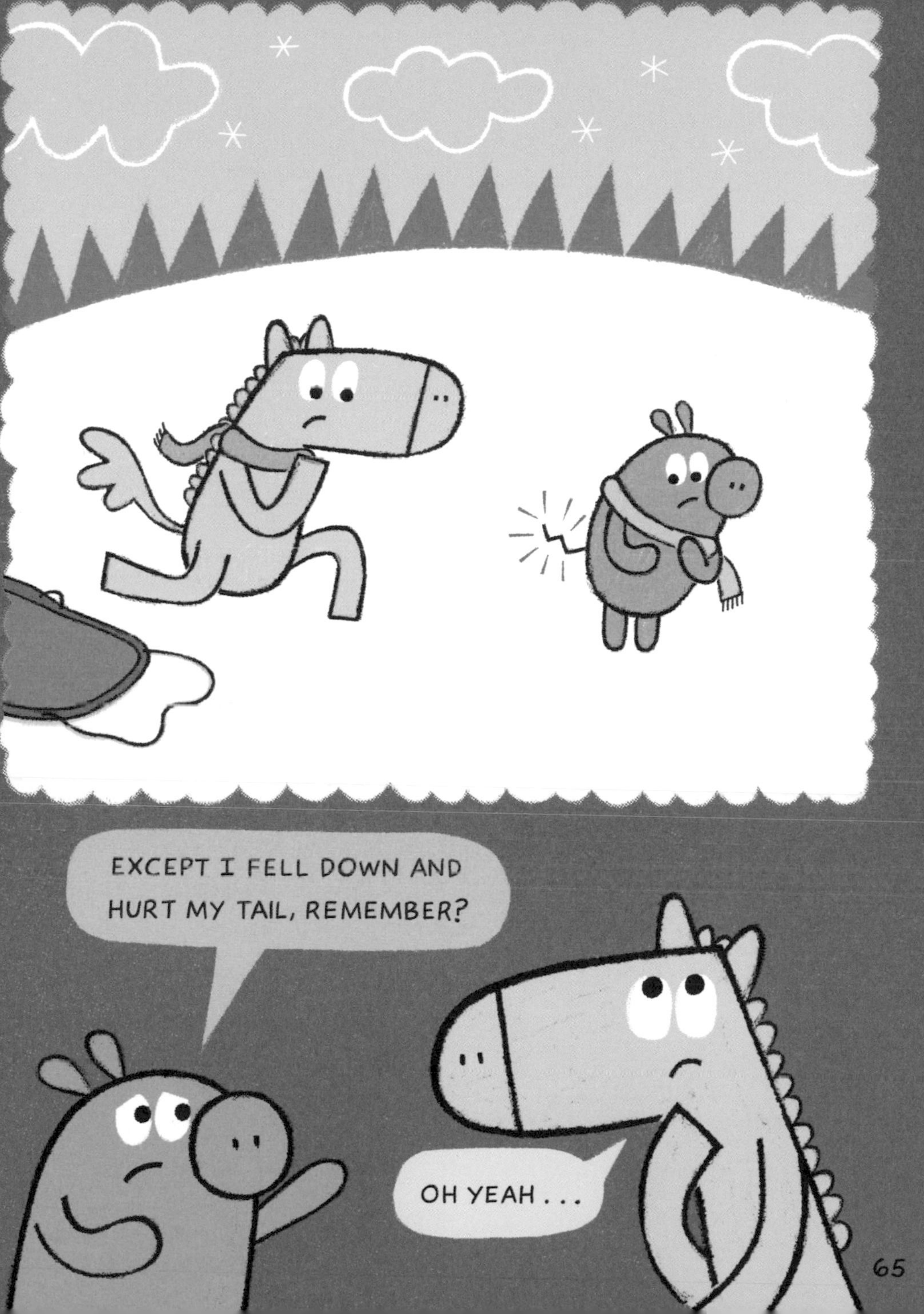
EXCEPT I FELL DOWN AND HURT MY TAIL, REMEMBER?
OH YEAH . . .

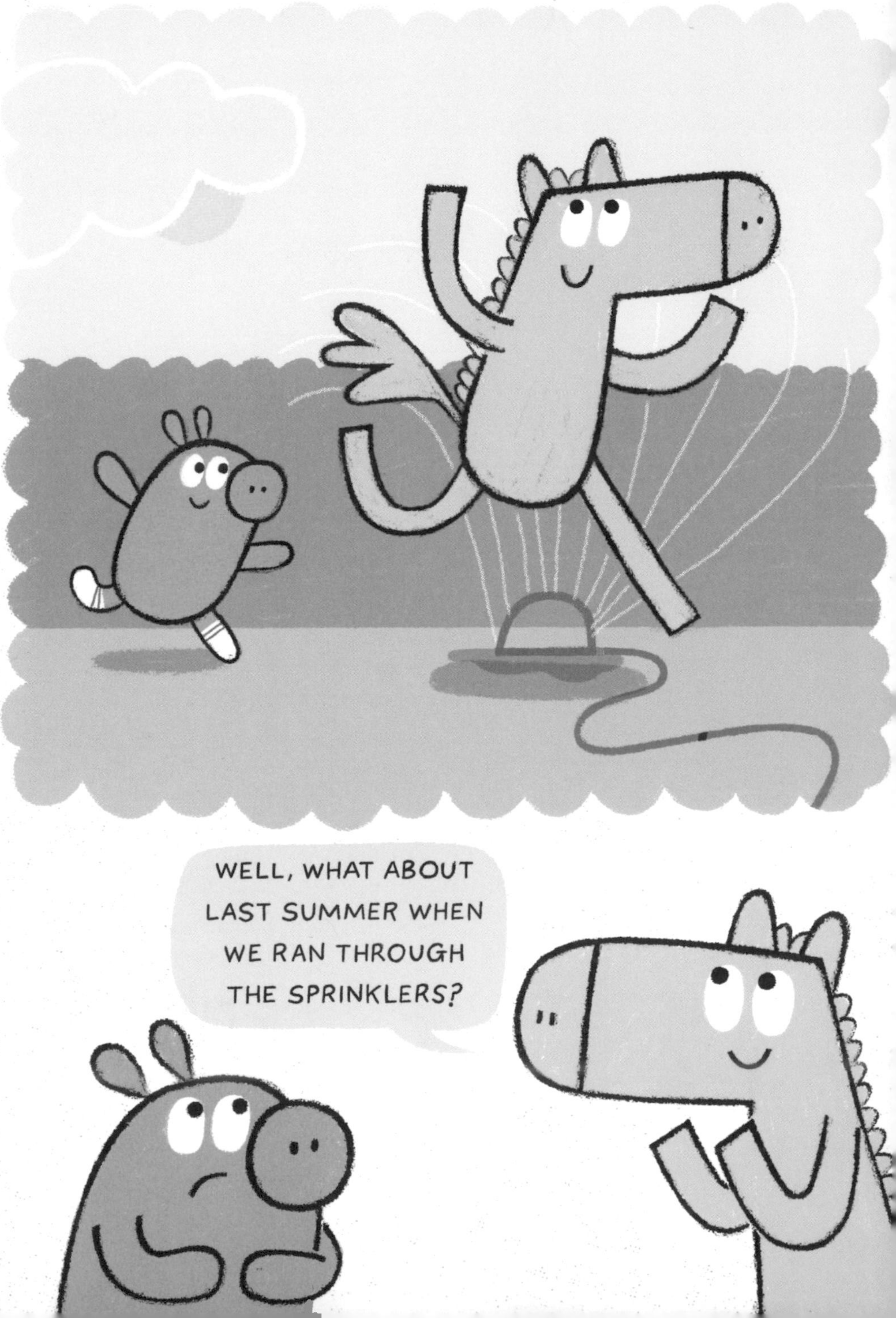
WELL, WHAT ABOUT LAST SUMMER WHEN WE RAN THROUGH THE SPRINKLERS?

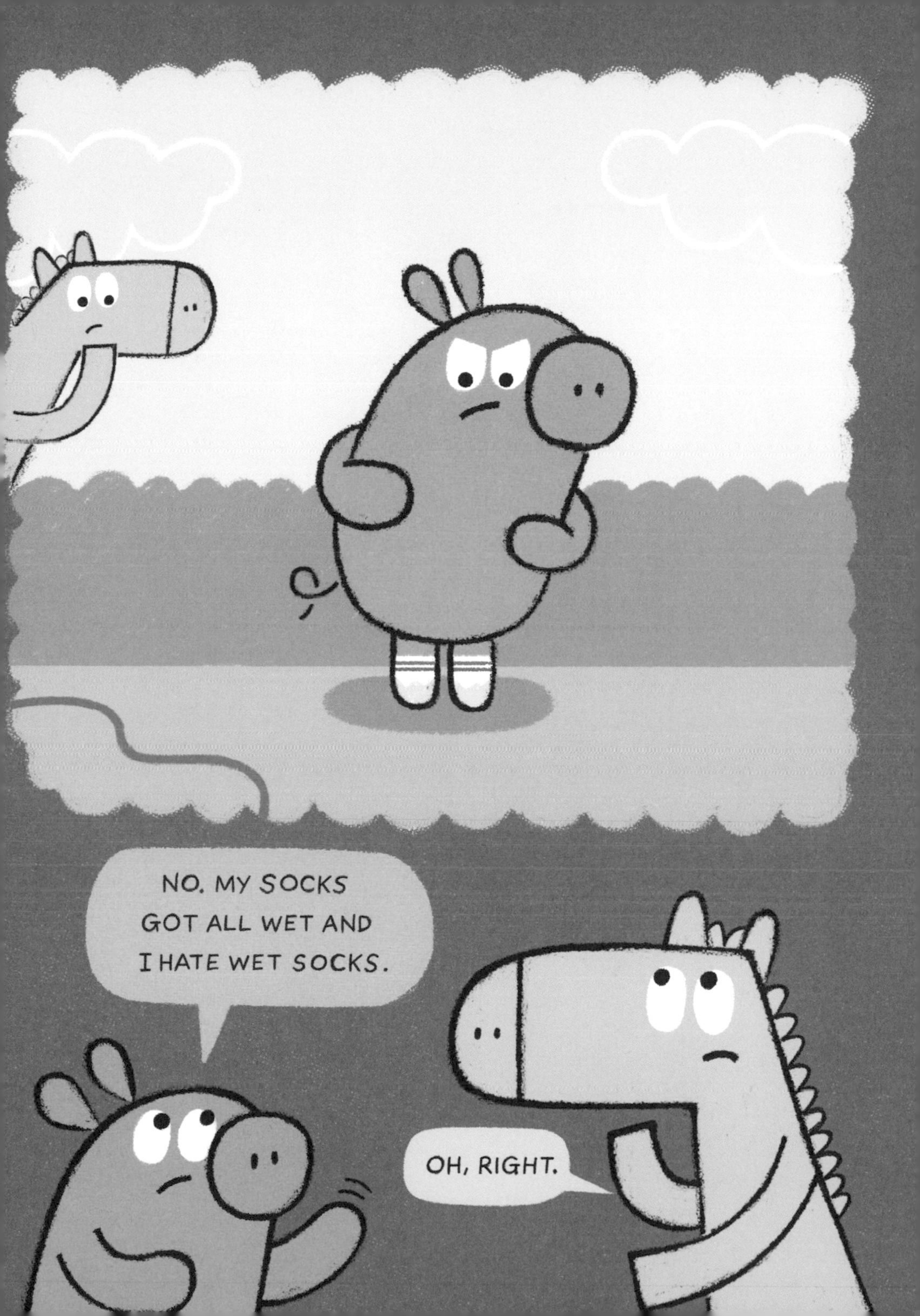
NO. MY SOCKS GOT ALL WET AND I HATE WET SOCKS.
OH, RIGHT.

WOW, YOU *ARE* BLUE.

YEAH . . .

WAIT . . .

I'VE GOT IT!

CARROT STICKS AND PEANUT BUTTER! *DELICIOUS!*

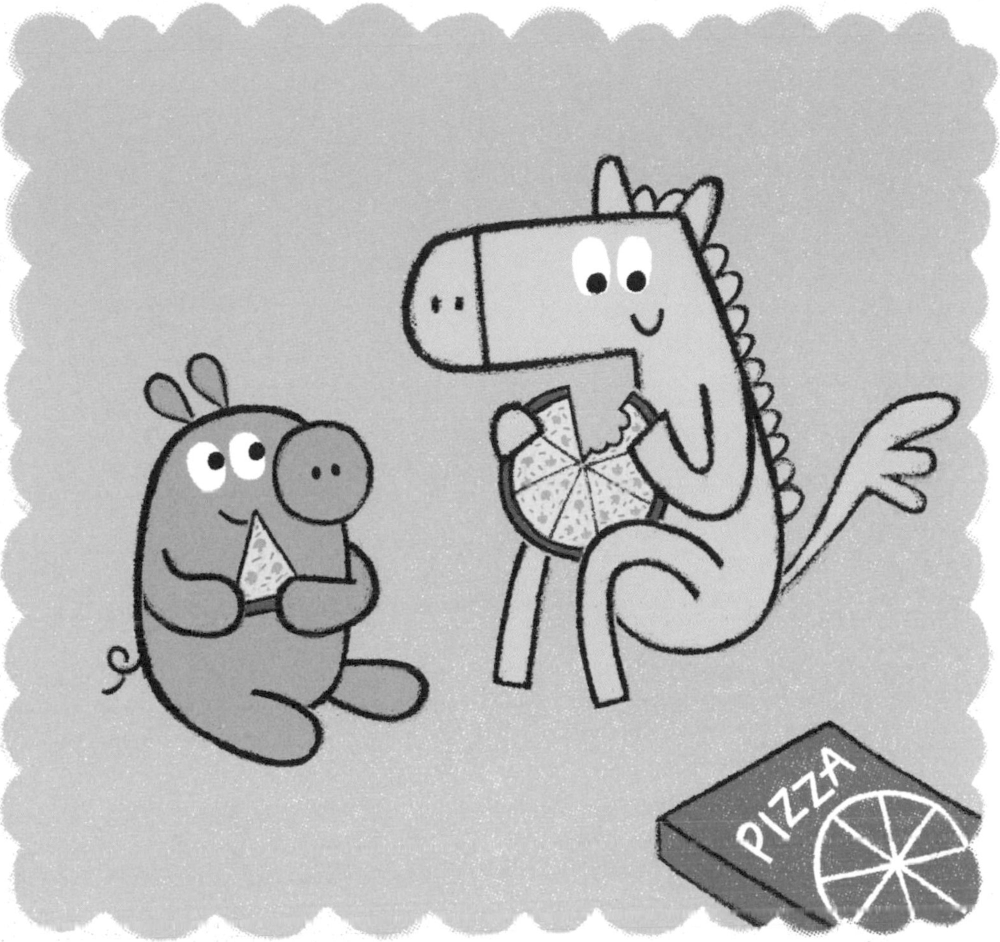
PIZZA

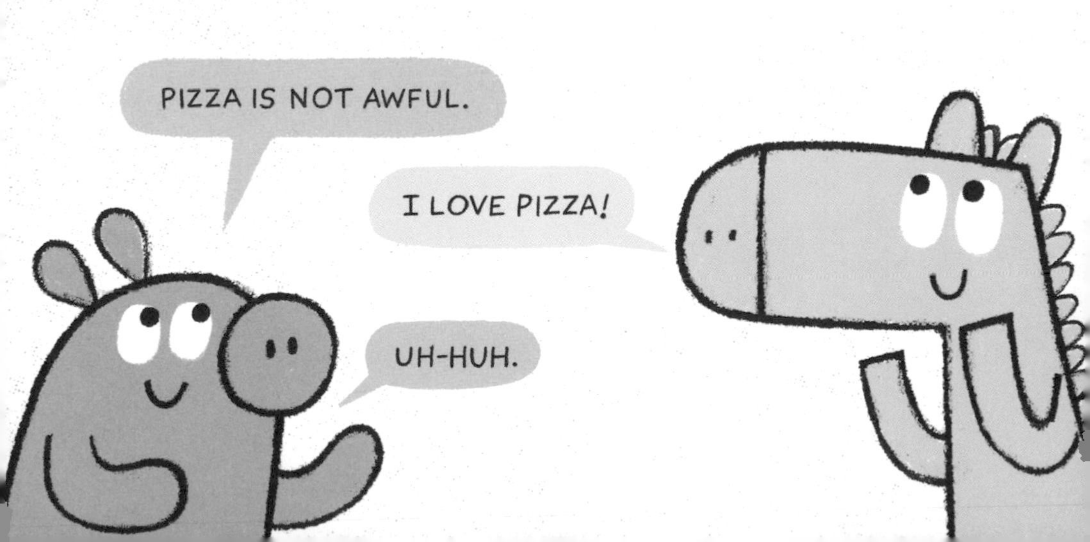
PIZZA IS NOT AWFUL.
I LOVE PIZZA!
UH-HUH.

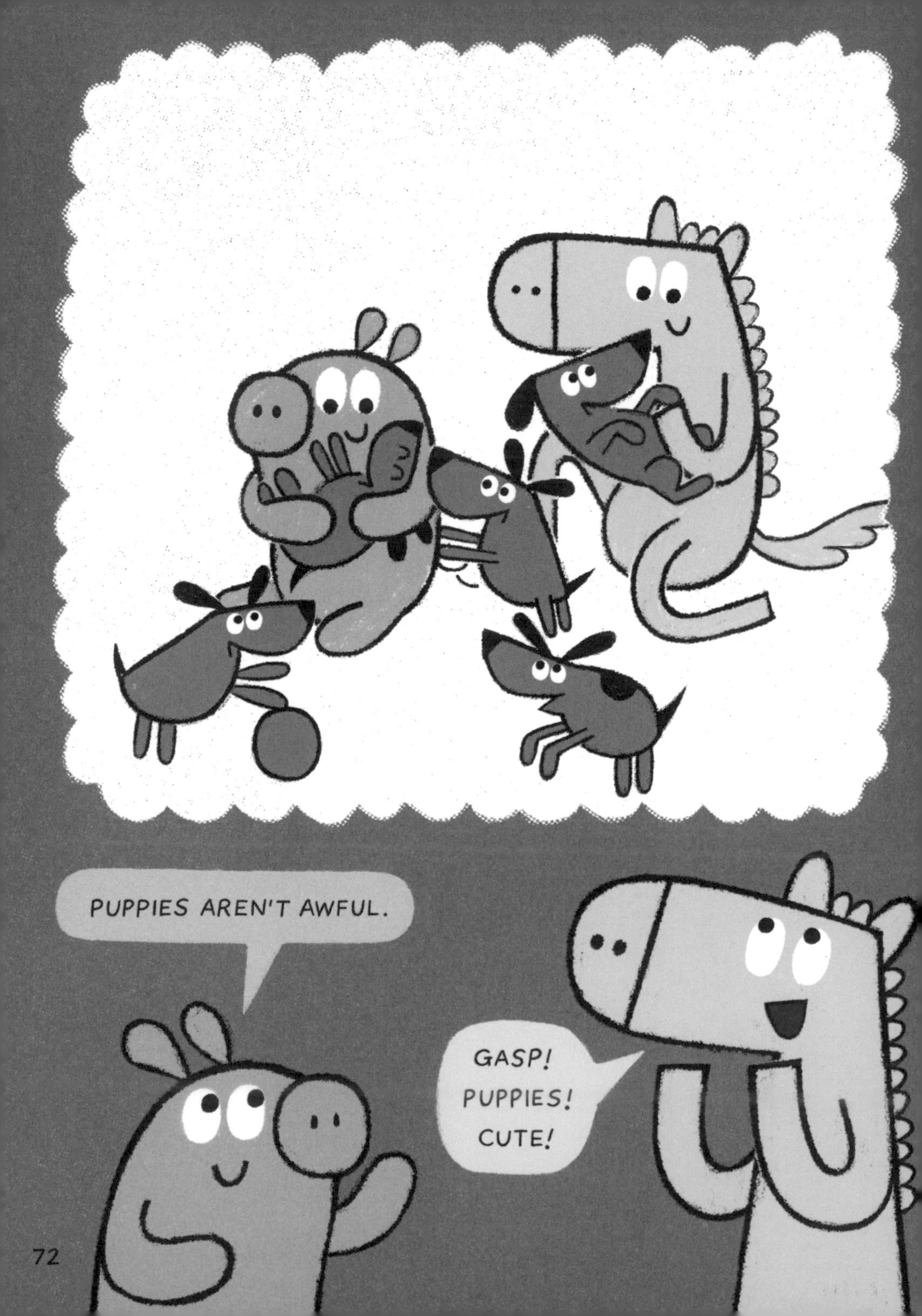
PUPPIES AREN'T AWFUL.
GASP! PUPPIES! CUTE!

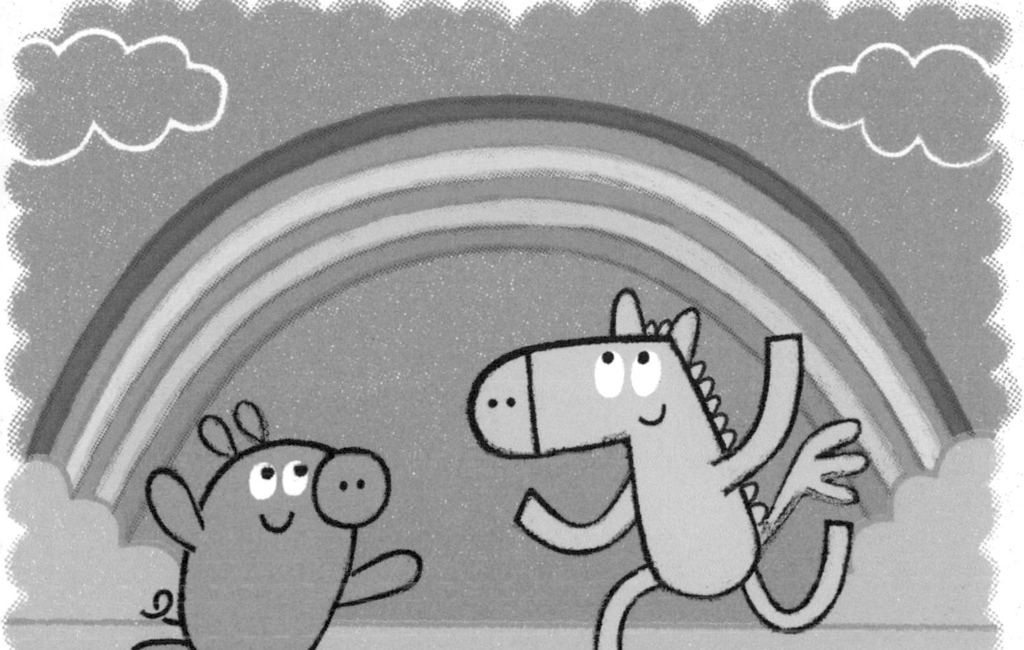

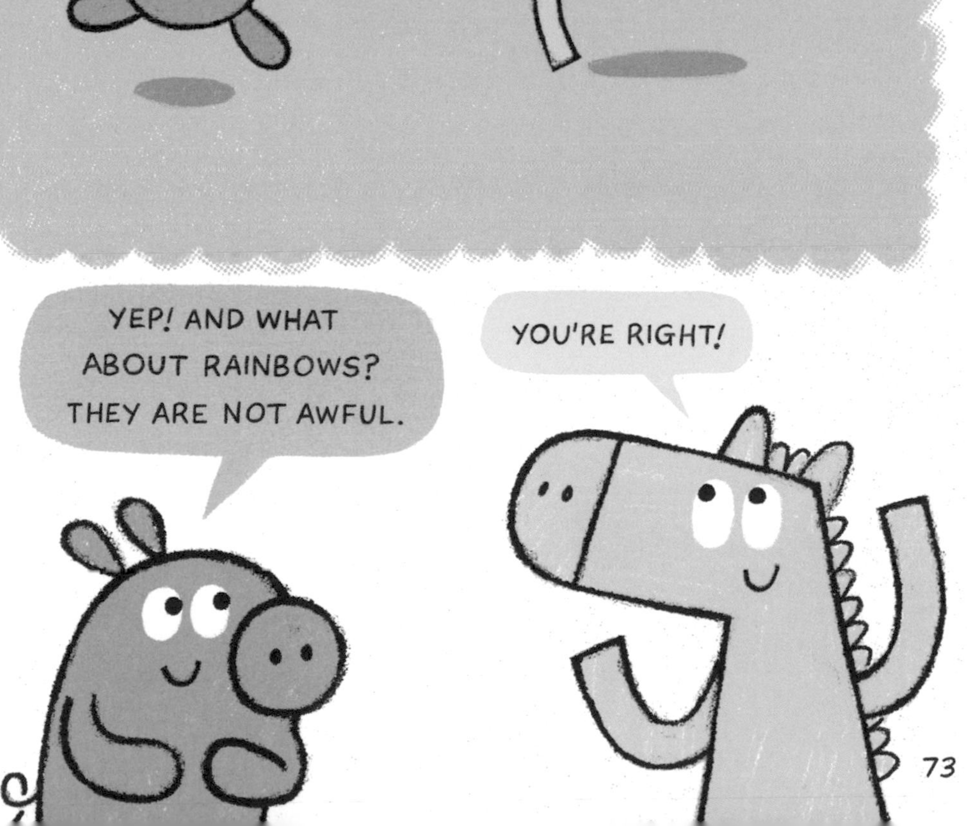
YEP! AND WHAT ABOUT RAINBOWS? THEY ARE NOT AWFUL.
YOU'RE RIGHT!

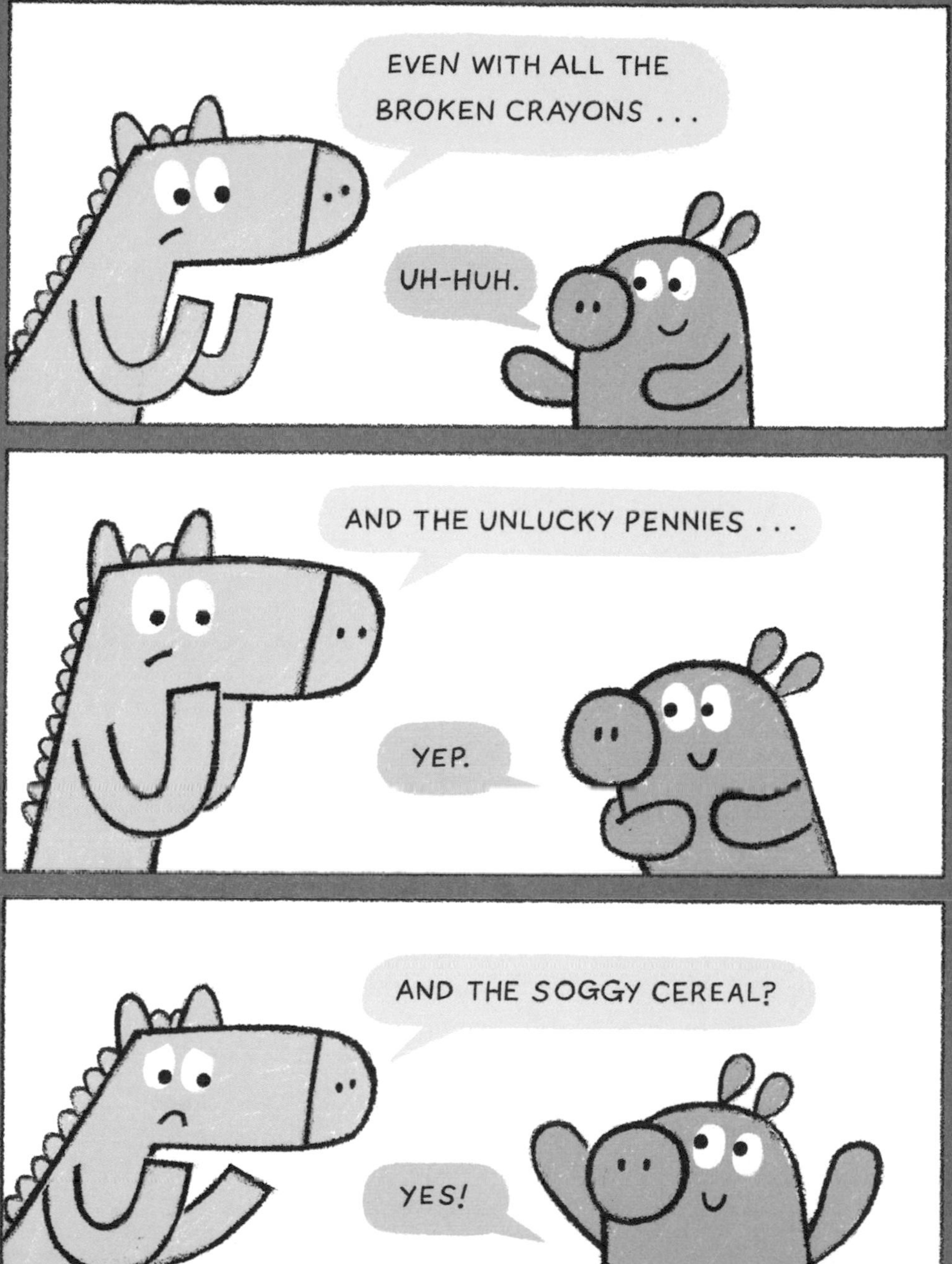
EVEN WITH ALL THE BROKEN CRAYONS . . .
UH-HUH.
AND THE UNLUCKY PENNIES . . .
YEP.
AND THE SOGGY CEREAL?
YES!

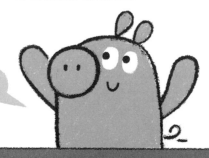

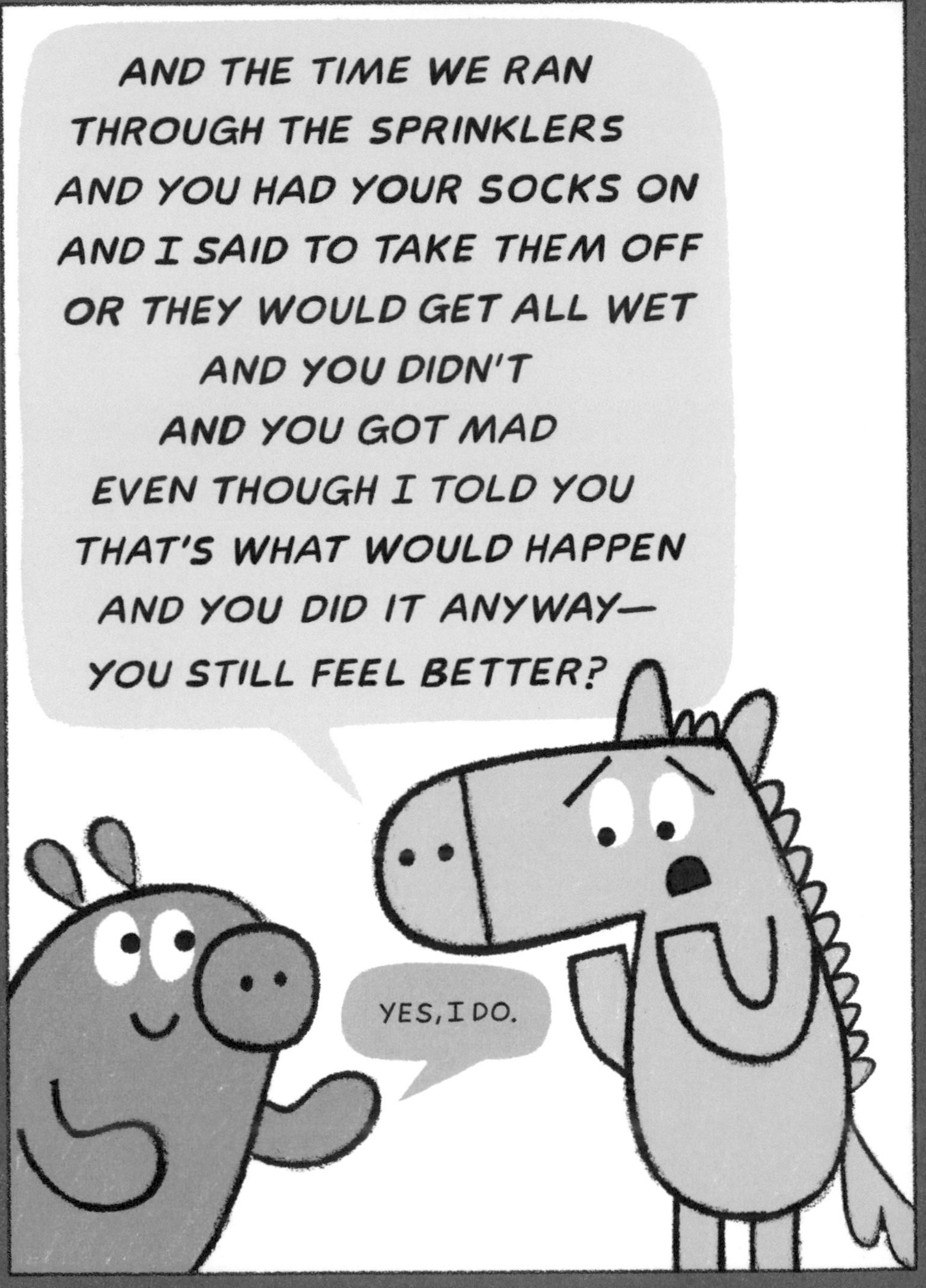
AND THE TIME WE RAN THROUGH THE SPRINKLERS AND YOU HAD YOUR SOCKS ON AND I SAID TO TAKE THEM OFF OR THEY WOULD GET ALL WET AND YOU DIDN'T AND YOU GOT MAD EVEN THOUGH I TOLD YOU THAT'S WHAT WOULD HAPPEN AND YOU DID IT ANYWAY— YOU STILL FEEL BETTER?
YES, I DO.

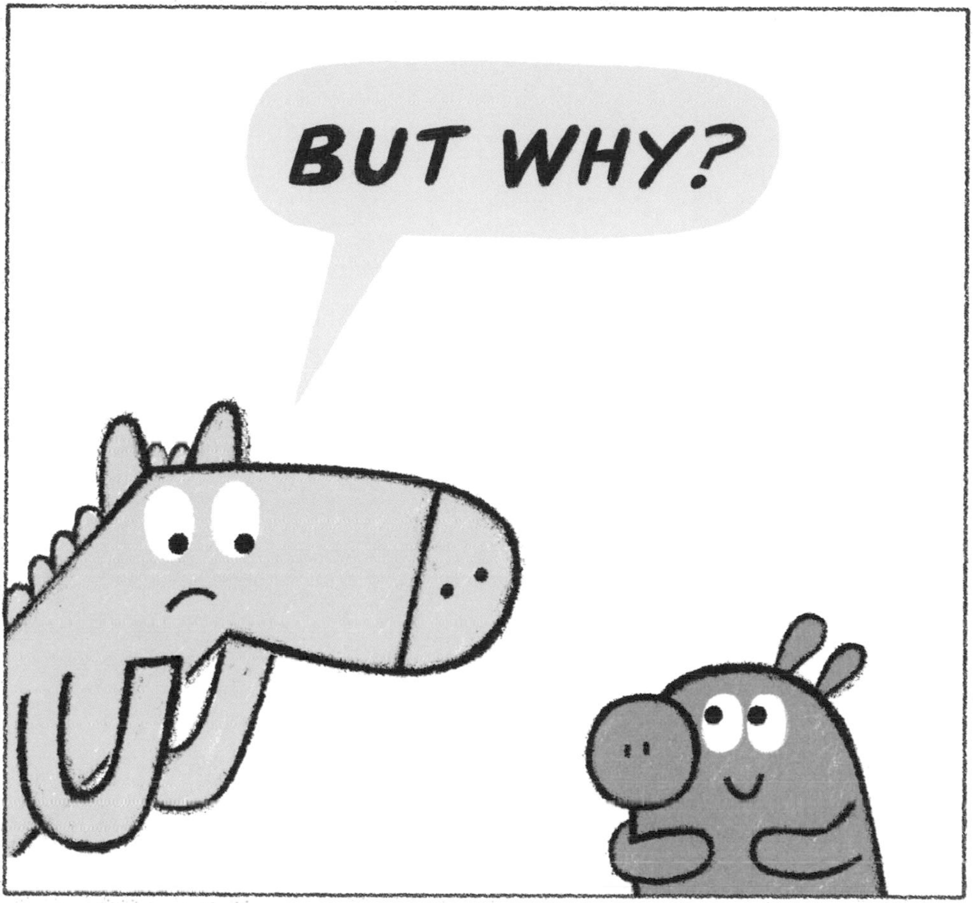
BUT WHY?

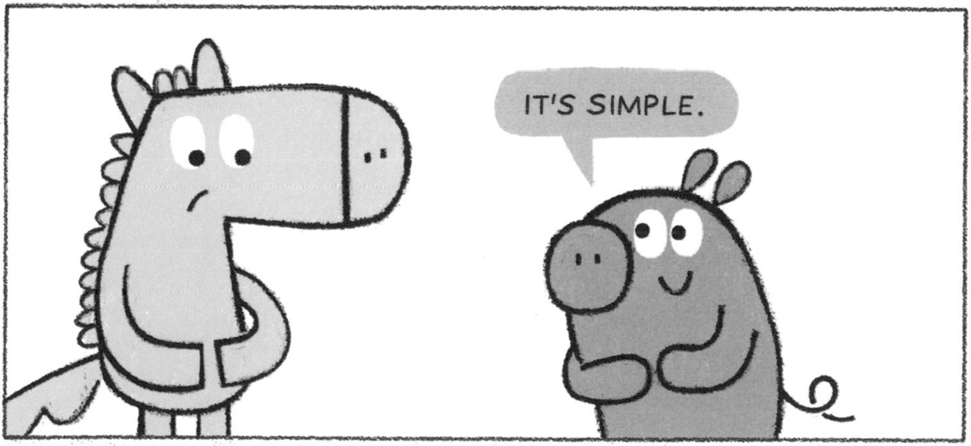
IT'S SIMPLE.

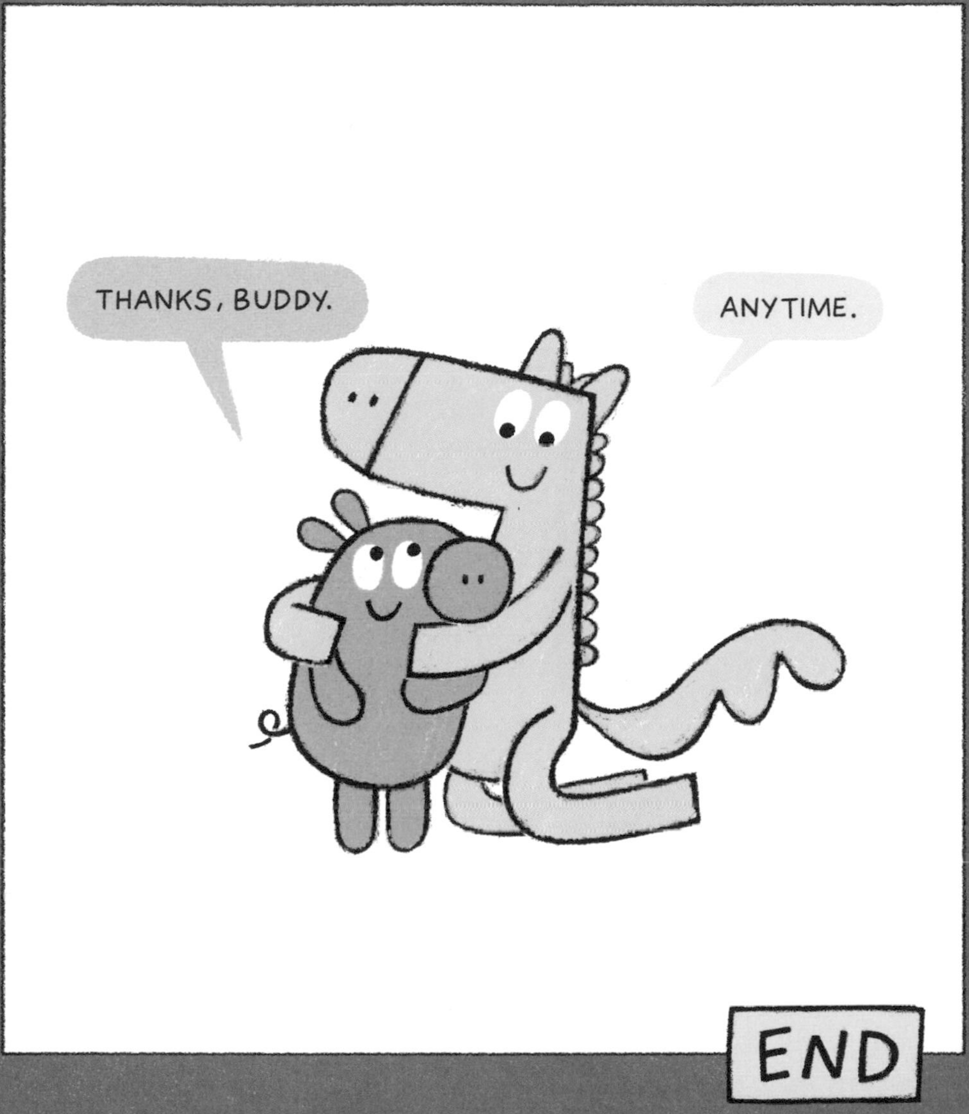
THANKS, BUDDY.
ANYTIME.
END

YOU CAN

DRAW BALONEY

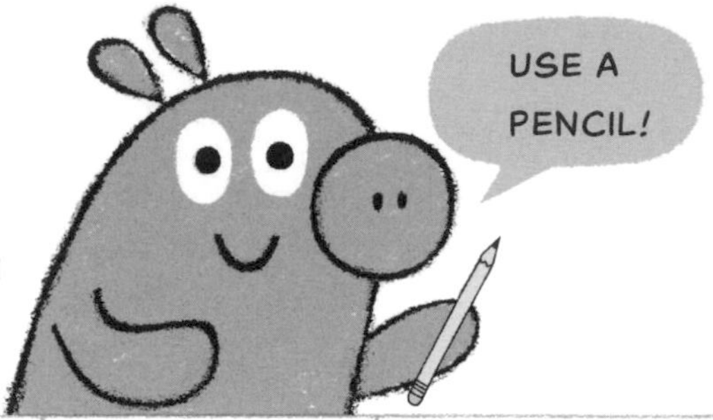
USE A PENCIL!

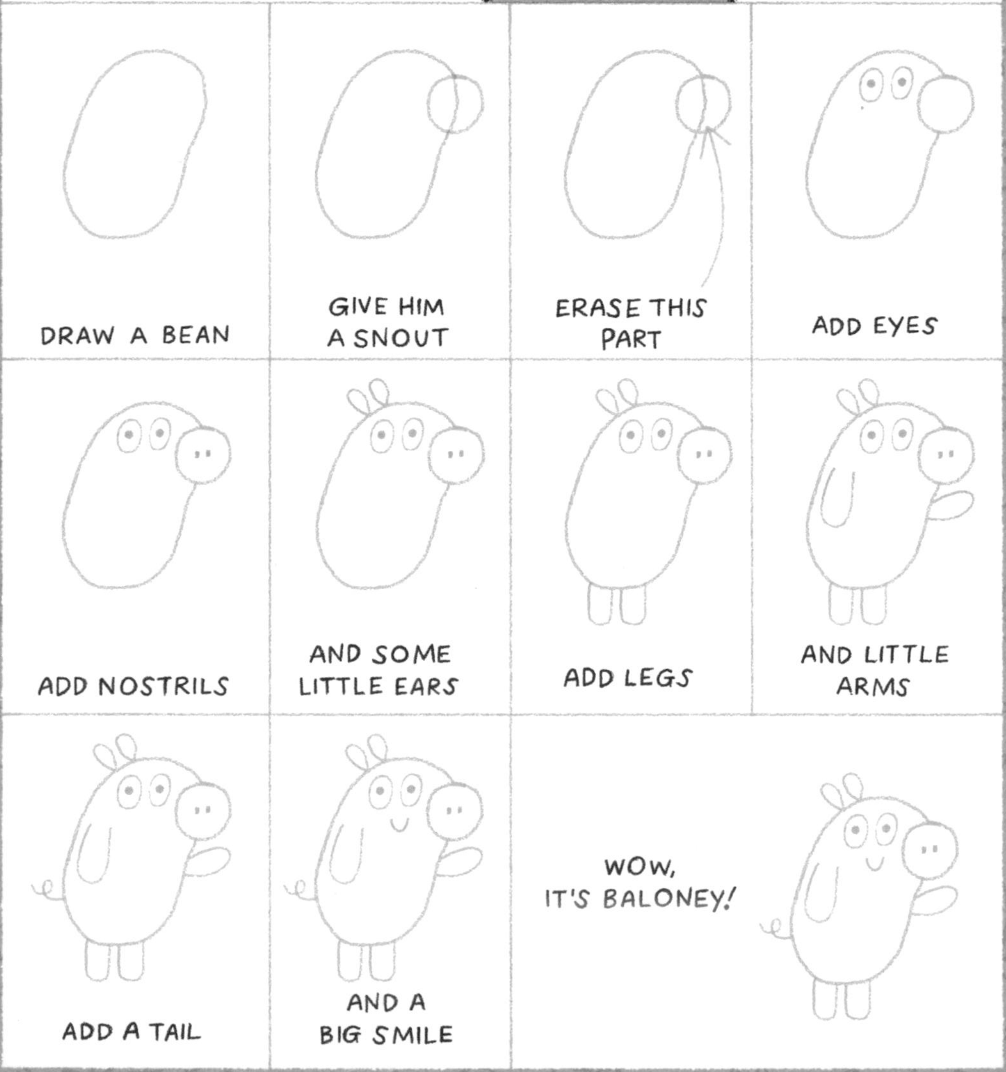
DRAW A BEAN
GIVE HIM A SNOUT
ERASE THIS PART
ADD EYES
ADD NOSTRILS
AND SOME LITTLE EARS
ADD LEGS
AND LITTLE ARMS
ADD A TAIL
AND A BIG SMILE
WOW, IT'S BALONEY!

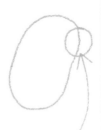

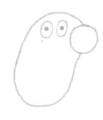

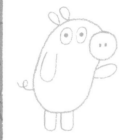

AND DRAW PEANUT TOO!

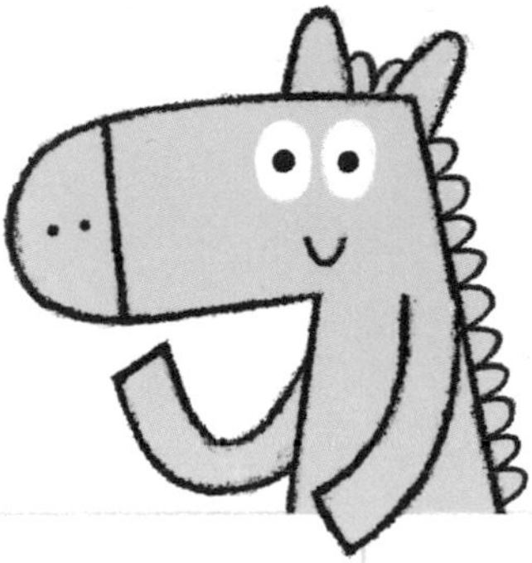

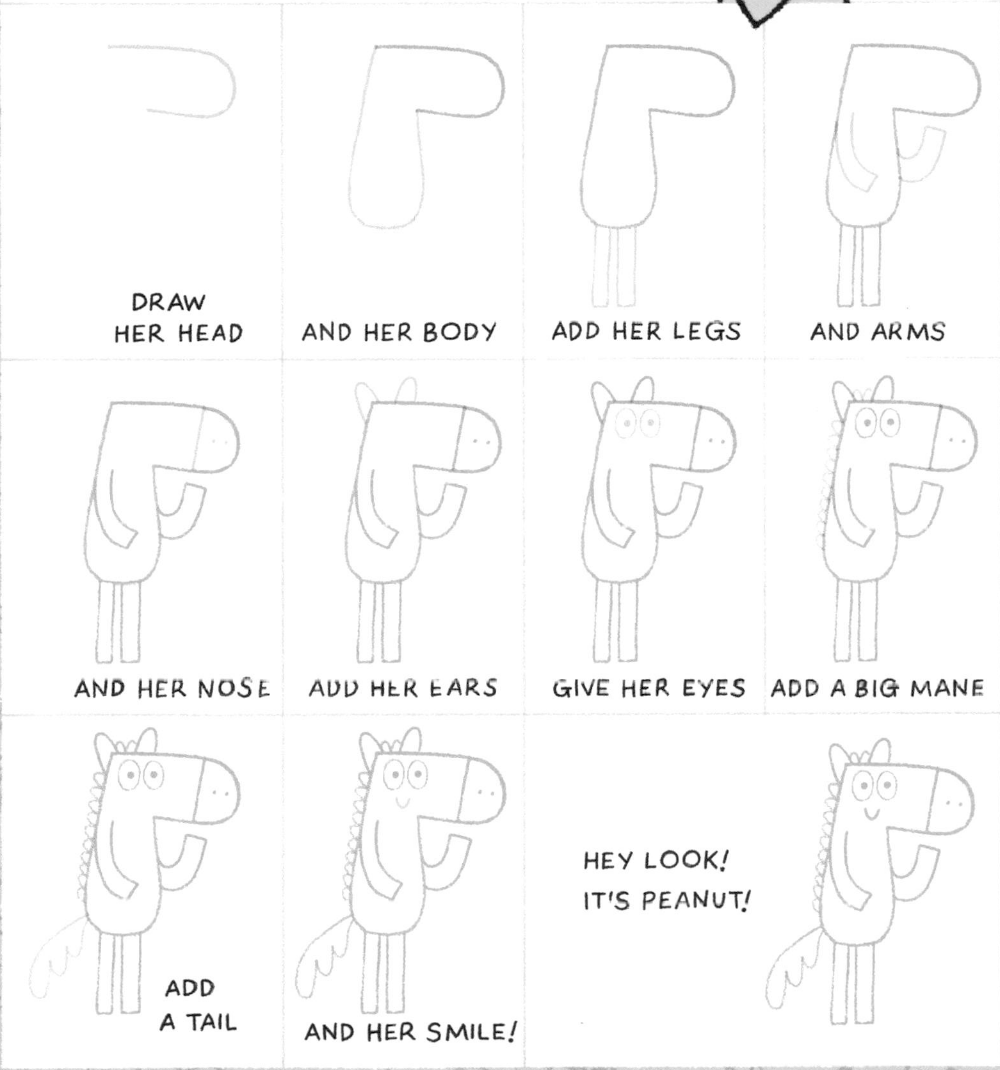
DRAW HER HEAD
AND HER BODY
ADD HER LEGS
AND ARMS
AND HER NOSE
ADD HER EARS
GIVE HER EYES
ADD A BIG MANE
ADD A TAIL
AND HER SMILE!
HEY LOOK! IT'S PEANUT!

DON'T FORGET TO

DRAW BIZZ

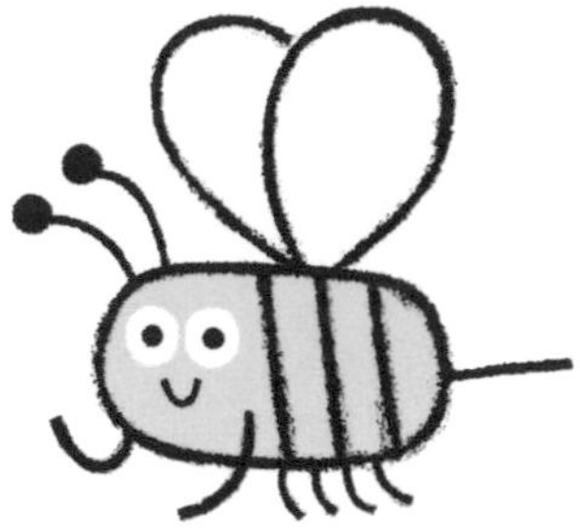

DRAW AN OVAL

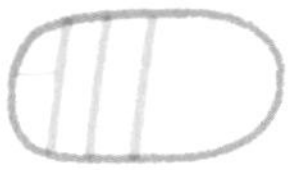

ADD STRIPES

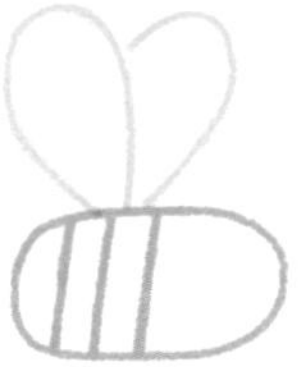

AND SOME WINGS

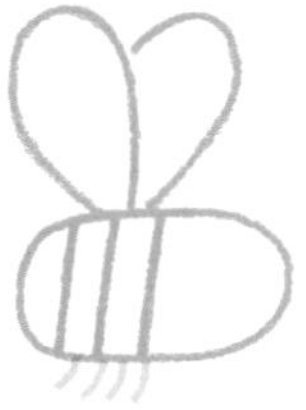

AND SOME TEENY LEGS

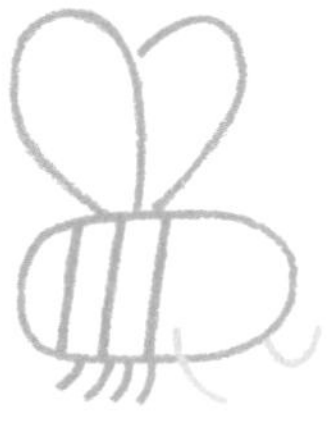

GIVE HER TWO ARMS

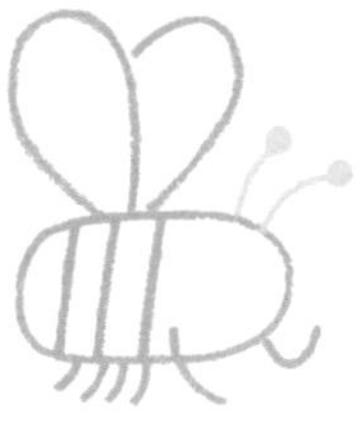

AND TWO ANTENNAE

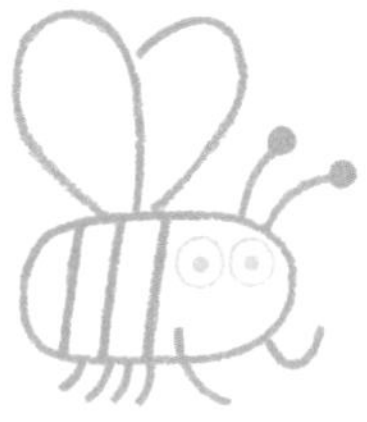

GIVE HER SOME EYES

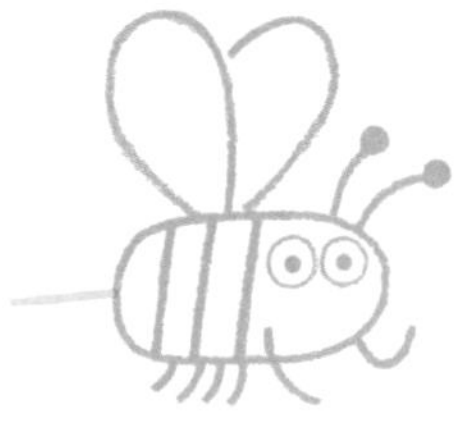

ADD HER STINGER

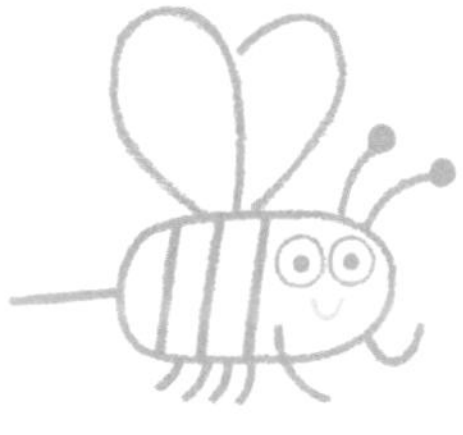

AND A BIG SMILE!

AND THAT'S BIZZ!

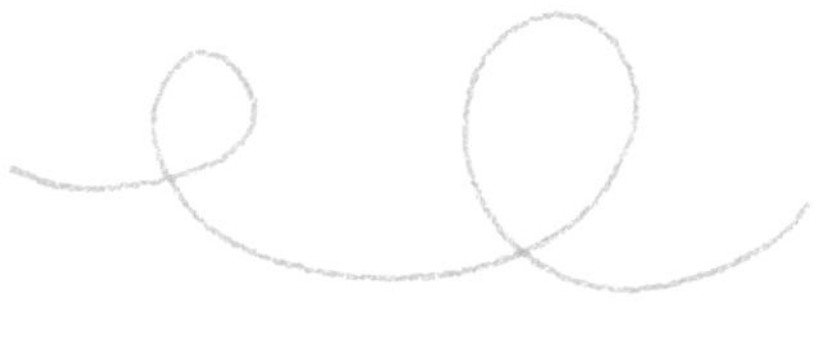

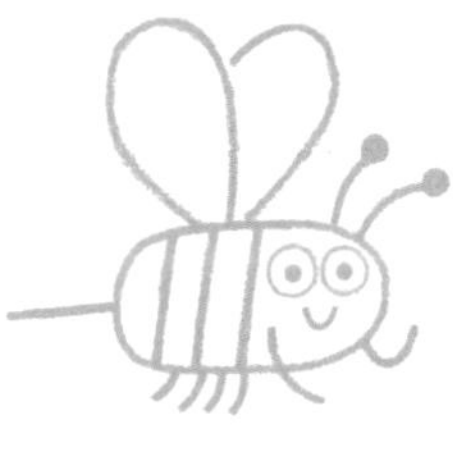

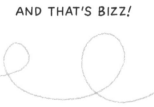

AND, YEAH, I GUESS
YOU MIGHT AS WELL

DRAW KRABBIT

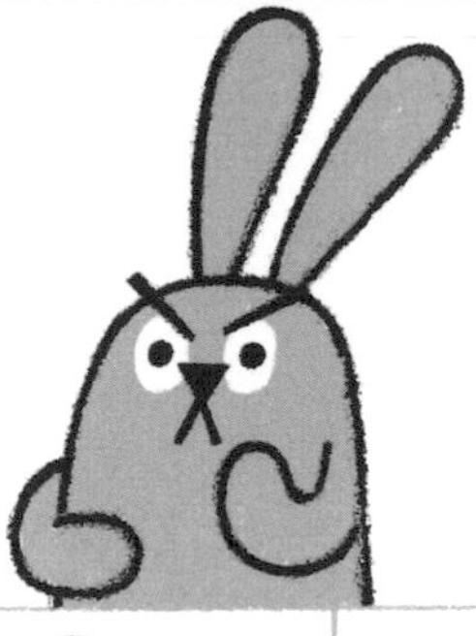

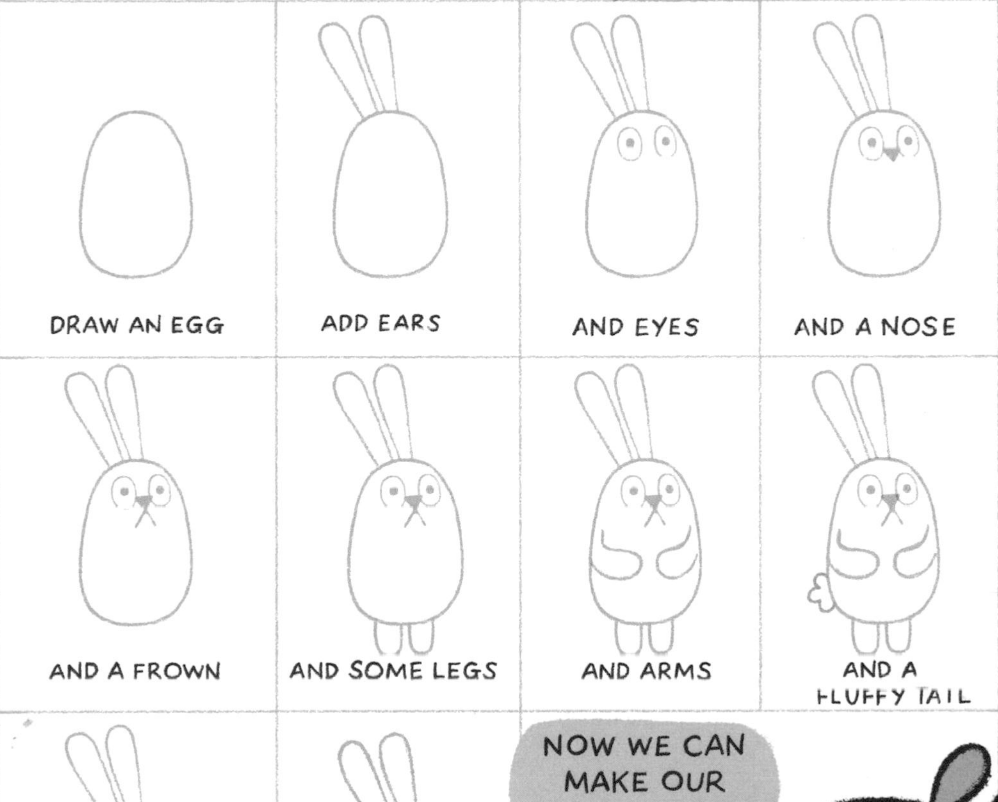

DRAW AN EGG

ADD EARS

AND EYES

AND A NOSE

AND A FROWN

AND SOME LEGS

AND ARMS

AND A FLUFFY TAIL

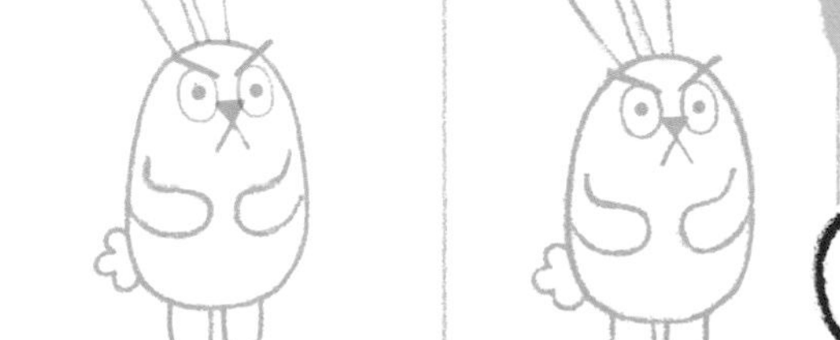

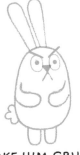

MAKE HIM GRUMPY

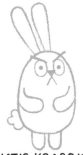

THAT'S KRABBIT!

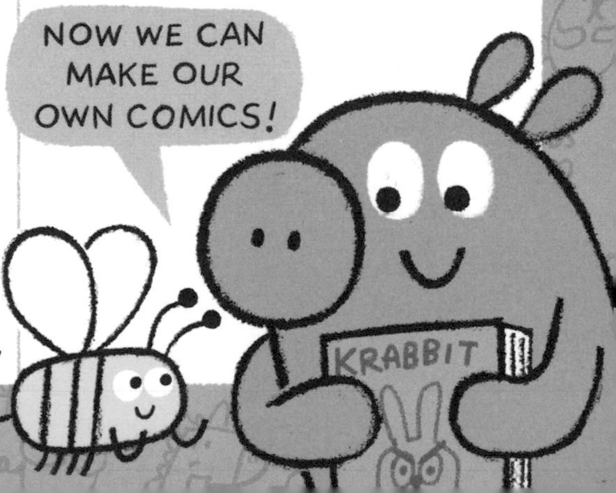
NOW WE CAN MAKE OUR OWN COMICS!
KRABBIT

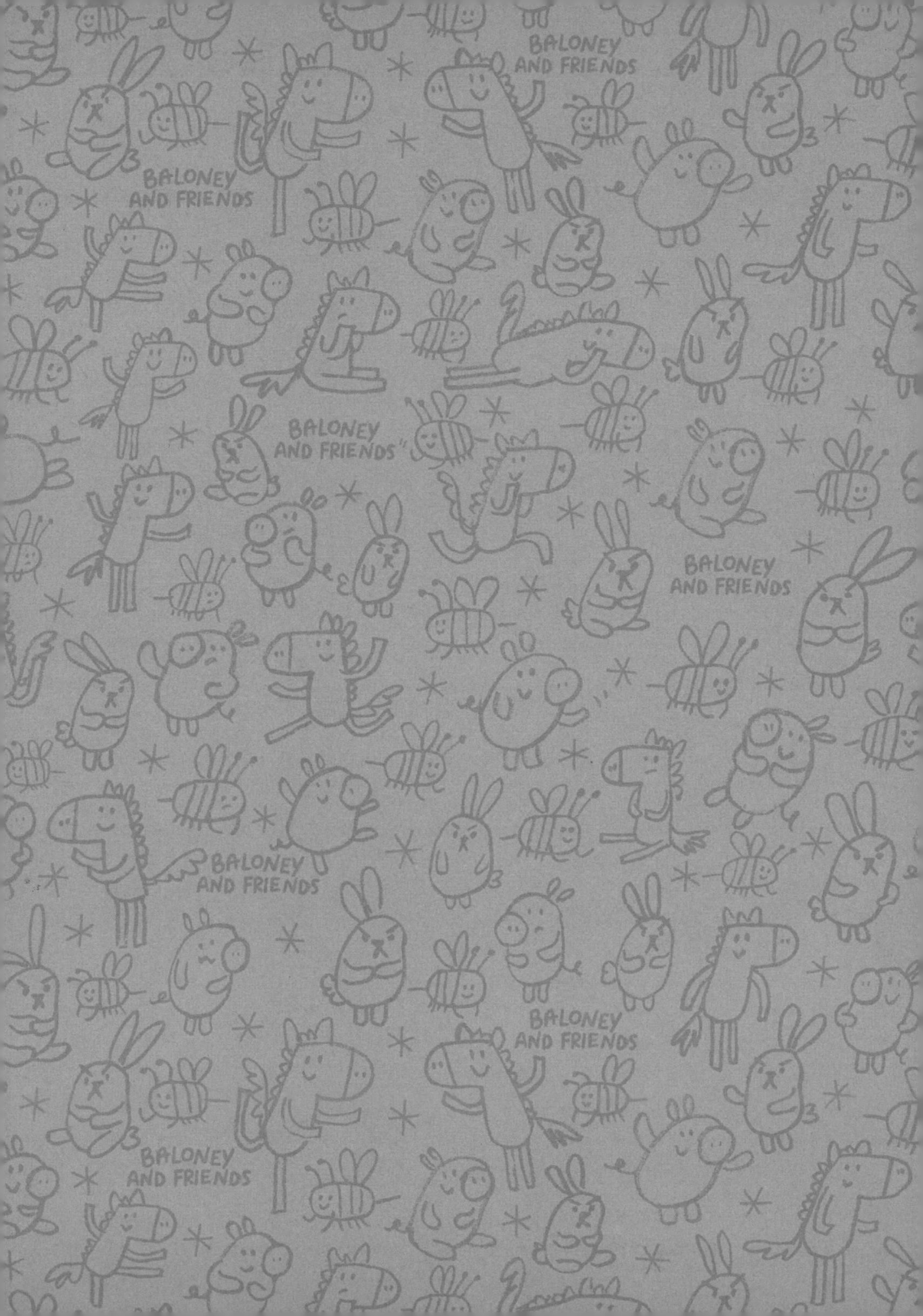
BALONEY AND FRIENDS
BALONEY AND FRIENDS
BALONEY AND FRIENDS
BALONEY AND FRIENDS
BALONEY AND FRIENDS
BALONEY AND FRIENDS
BALONEY AND FRIENDS